From Italy
with Love

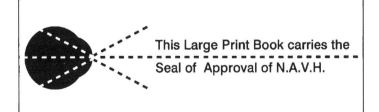

This Large Print Book carries the
Seal of Approval of N.A.V.H.

Book One

From Italy with Love

Motivated by Letters, Two Women
Travel to Italian Cities and Find Love

Gail Gaymer Martin
DiAnn Mills

Thorndike Press • Waterville, Maine

Published in 2004 by arrangement with
Barbour Publishing, Inc.

Thorndike Press® Large Print Christian Fiction.

The tree indicium is a trademark of Thorndike Press.

The text of this Large Print edition is unabridged.
Other aspects of the book may vary from the original edition.

Set in 16 pt. Plantin by Minnie B. Raven.

Printed in the United States on permanent paper.

Library of Congress Cataloging-in-Publication Data

From Italy with love : motivated by letters, two women travel
  to Italian cities and find love/ Gail Gaymer Martin . . .
  (et al.].
      p. cm.
   Originally published in 2003 in one v.
   Contents: bk 1. An open door / by Gail Gaymer Martin.
The lure of Capri / by DiAnn Mills — bk. 2. To Florence
with love / by Melanie Panagiotopoulos. Roman holiday /
by Lois M. Richer.
   ISBN 0-7862-7079-9 (v. 1; lg. print : hc : alk. paper)
   1. Love stories, American.   2. Americans — Italy —
Fiction.   3. Women travelers — Fiction.   4. Italy —
Fiction.   5. Large type books.   I. Martin, Gail Gaymer,
1937–
PS374.L6F76 2004
  813´.085083245—dc22   2004058067

From Italy
with Love

As the Founder/CEO of NAVH, the only national health agency solely devoted to those who, although not totally blind, have an eye disease which could lead to serious visual impairment, I am pleased to recognize Thorndike Press★ as one of the leading publishers in the large print field.

Founded in 1954 in San Francisco to prepare large print textbooks for partially seeing children, NAVH became the pioneer and standard setting agency in the preparation of large type.

Today, those publishers who meet our standards carry the prestigious "Seal of Approval" indicating high quality large print. We are delighted that Thorndike Press is one of the publishers whose titles meet these standards. We are also pleased to recognize the significant contribution Thorndike Press is making in this important and growing field.

Lorraine H. Marchi, L.H.D.
Founder/CEO
NAVH

★ Thorndike Press encompasses the following imprints: Thorndike, Wheeler, Walker and Large Print Press.

An Open Door

Gail Gaymer Martin

Therefore, as God's chosen people,
holy and dearly loved,
clothe yourselves with compassion,
kindness, humility, gentleness and patience.
Bear with each other and forgive
whatever grievances
you may have against one another.
Forgive as the Lord forgave you.
And over all these virtues put on love,
which binds them all together
in perfect unity.
COLOSSIANS 3:12–14

Prologue

Steffi Rosetti clenched the black-banded letter in her trembling hands. Tears pooled in her eyes until they escaped and rolled down her cheeks. Anger? Sorrow? Confusion?

Her senses had numbed since she opened the letter, postmarked Venice, Italy, and the message tumbled through her mind like a grocer's can goods display falling to the floor. The clatter of words and emotions rattled all the way to her heart.

Steffi dragged her gaze, again, to the signature. Donata Rosetti. A grandmother she'd never met. The mother of her father she'd never known. Deep grief rolled over her. Grief . . . and what? Apprehension? Hope?

Steffi lowered her gaze to the graceful flourish of her penmanship, the uncertain wording, the unbelievable love that soared from the paper and wondered if she'd misunderstood, perhaps misread. Again she followed the sentences word by word.

11

My Dearest Steffi,

I pray you do not destroy this letter before reading it. I have asked a dear friend to search for you on, what he calls, the Internet. I have long lost your mother's address, having no need for it . . . under the circumstances.

I am sending you love and sad news from Italy. Though I promised your dear father to keep from his business, he has gone to God, and now I do what my heart has longed to do for years. I find you. Words cannot say what is in my heart. I ask God to bring you to visit me so I may tell you about your father and about your relatives in this beautiful country. If you find it in your heart to answer my simple letter, I will be most grateful and give to God many praise for His goodness. A visit by you to your father's homeland is my largest dream.

I am sorry to tell you of your father's early death, but it gives me opportunity to share with you my love and prayers for these many years. Please say you will come to Venice so I can meet you in person and hold your hand in mine.

With love from Italy,
Donata Rosetti

Tears dripped to the cream-colored stationery, smudging the ink into dark puddles, and Steffi wiped her eyes with the back of her hand. She'd known so little of her father, only that he'd left her and her mother to return to Italy when Steffi was two. Sometimes when she delved deep into her memory, she thought she remembered a handsome, dark-haired man who held her in his arms so many years ago.

But reality struck her with the truth. She'd once found a photograph — one her mother hadn't destroyed — and hid it in her treasure box. Though she loved her mother deeply, Steffi longed to know what had really happened. Why had her father abandoned her?

Please say you will come to Venice so I can meet you in person and hold your hand in mine. The words sent an unearthly prickle up Steffi's arms. The coincidence tangled in her thoughts. Her magazine editor had assigned her to cover the Italian designers' autumn and winter collections, and she would leave in another week for Italy. Not Venice, but Milan . . . and if she knew geography, Venice was not too far away.

And was the invitation a coincidence? Steffi knew God worked miracles. If the Lord could move mountains and turn sin-

13

ners into pillars of salt, surely He could bring two people together — seeming strangers from two distant lands. But would the Lord heal Steffi's heart?

The thought sent fear skittering through her chest. Another disappointment. Another dashed hope. The trip to Milan flashed through her mind. Certainly she could add a couple of days to her venture. She could take a train to Venice.

The question was, would she?

Chapter 1

Steffi Rosetti gripped the handle of her carry-on case and headed for baggage claim. At least that's what she hoped when she saw the word *bagagli*. Other passengers were heading in that direction, so she plastered on a confident expression and trudged through the busy Milan airport.

With a relieved sigh, she found baggage claim, gathered her pieces of luggage, and made her way through security and customs. Outside, she maneuvered her bags toward the long line at the taxi stand.

The smell of fuel and warm concrete filled the air as she jostled her way to the end of the line. Steffi disliked this part of travel most. Long lines at the airport, passing through customs, and waiting for cabs were the worst part of travel. She'd done it before on a smaller scale, traveling for her work as feature writer for the fashion magazine, *Mode*.

Inching along, she bided her time, listening to the people around her talking with the speed of a race car driver, their voices riding on the air in a jumble of unique rhythms, syllables, rolled Rs, and punctuated with animated motions.

The line moved forward again. Now only one couple waited in front of her. Steffi drew in a long breath, knowing she'd be next.

"Scusi!"

She heard a male voice and turned, thinking the man was speaking to her. Instead, the impeccably dressed young man was flagging the taxi-attendant. Steffi watched the man move to the young man's side, and they stood talking. The young man was obviously a seasoned traveler. He looked sophisticated, in brown slacks and beige wool sport coat, a brown hanky in the breast pocket. His sport shirt in earth tones lay open at the neck, giving him a jaunty look, like a man who knew fashion.

Steffi looked down at her faded jeans topped by an oversized sweatshirt and cringed. She had flown from the United States to cover a designer fashion show, and she looked like she'd won a competition at the state fair log rolling contest. She shrugged to herself. Who cared how she looked? All she needed to do was write a compelling article about the latest fashions.

16

Steffi noted the young man's impatience as he huffed and paced beside the taxi attendant. His voice punctuated the air. *"Vorrei un tassi. Presto!"* With a subtle motion, the young man slipped paper money into the attendant's hand. She felt a frown settle on her face, wondering why he'd paid the man.

Before she had a chance to contemplate, the attendant hurried to her side. *"Scusi,* Signorina. The signor is in great need of the next taxi."

"He what?" She turned her head to flash a scowl at the young man who averted his gaze, obviously noticing her annoyed expression.

Crimping the fingertips of his right hand, he flexed his wrist. *"Grazie.* It is urgent, he says. You will have the next taxi. *Capisce?"*

Steffi stood her ground. She wasn't born yesterday. The money had been a bribe to help the man move ahead in line, she figured. She riveted her gaze to his. "No. The next taxi is *mine."* She arched an eyebrow and stared at the man.

The attendant shrugged and stepped over to the young man who was now watching her with curiosity.

Steffi's shoulders tensed, and her pulse

quickened, curious to see what would happen next. As she waited, shame settled over her. Perhaps the young man had a real emergency. The attendant had said it was urgent. Where was her compassion? Where was her Christian upbringing?

When the attendant glanced her way, Steffi beckoned him over. "If the man has an emergency, I'll be happy to share a taxi."

"Sì," he said, taking a step away.

Steffi grabbed his sleeve. "If he's going in my direction."

As she finished her statement, a cab rolled to a stop. The attendant opened the door and she slipped in. He spoke to the driver and hurried away. In a moment, the impatient young man slid in beside her.

"*Grazie,*" he said, giving her a nod. He leaned over the seat toward the driver. "Jolly Hotel Touring."

The driver shifted into gear, and the taxi pulled away.

Steffi gave the gentleman a puzzled look. "That's where I'm going," she mumbled, not knowing if the man understood English.

He laughed. "You're American."

She heard his Midwest dialect and irritation rose up her back. "Yes." She folded her hands in her lap and squirmed in the corner. She'd been duped by an American to share a cab, and she didn't like it one bit.

They rode in silence while she gazed through the windows at the wonderful sights that flashed past — buildings embedded in history and adorned with ornate facades, fresco moldings, and piazzas with magnificent statuary and fountains.

At a red light, her pulse skittered, seeing a unique art form that spanned both sides of the median. On one side a towering threaded needle rose from the ground while a strand of yellow, green, and red intercepted the needle's eye in a loop, then dangled to the ground. On the opposite side of the street, two strands of thread rose from a small fountain pool and knotted at the end. The whimsy was an amazing tribute to Milan, the center of the fashion industry. She nearly commented to her fellow passenger, but caught herself. The young man shuffled through papers in his lap, and she decided to curtail a taxi-ride friendship.

The hotel came into view off the via Turati, a pink and gray concrete structure with a black overhang sporting the hotel's name. When they came to a stop, the driver unloaded the baggage, and Steffi paid the driver and toted hers inside.

At the registration desk her irritation with the young man faded as her mind filled with her purpose in Milan. Covering the new couture fashions for *Mode* was a coup for her career, but more than that, her thoughts settled on the letter she carried in her shoulder bag. The letter from her grandmother had weighed on her heart — a grandmother she'd never met, yet a woman whose sadness and grief rose from the words on the stationery.

Steffi had fought the idea of visiting the woman . . . her father's mother, but curiosity and compassion nudged her to reconsider. Steffi's mother had filled her head with negative comments about her father, a man who'd forsaken them when Steffi was young. What could her grandmother tell her to make things better? How could the older woman excuse her son's abandonment of his family in the United States? The questions weighted Steffi's mind as she clasped her key and rolled her luggage to the elevator.

The young man from the taxi had vanished, and Steffi was relieved. Yet curiosity infiltrated her thoughts. He was an American, staying at the same hotel. A strange coincidence, she thought. No matter, she hoped she never saw him again.

She erased the last thought as her inquiring mind poked her with questions.

Paul DiAngelo dropped his bag on the bed and set his tote on the luggage rack. He gazed around the room — nothing luxurious, but pleasant. After tugging off his sport jacket and hanging it on the chair back, Paul slipped off his shoes and sank into a chair, thinking about his trip from the airport. He'd acted like a pompous jerk, slipping the taxi attendant money to move ahead in line. Why? He was no better than anyone else, but he'd watched others do it and he thought he would give it a try.

He'd certainly made a bad impression on the woman he'd met on the ride to the hotel, and he was disconcerted when he learned she was staying at the same hotel. For some reason, he figured she was a farmer's daughter returning home from somewhere or perhaps her family owned a small vineyard. Her casual attire — the baggy sweatshirt and jeans and her hair tied back in a ponytail — had thrown him off course. What he had noticed was her pretty face . . . until she glowered at him.

The vision made him laugh. Who was

21

she? And why was she in Milan? His stomach rumbled, and he put his clothes away for the week's stay. From another bag, he pulled out his camera equipment. He'd carried it on the airplane rather than take a chance on having it misplaced in baggage or damaged. Cameras were his livelihood. Paul approached his new position with *Mode* filled with excitement and a sense of challenge. Shooting the new fashions in Milan would be his first assignment for the magazine, and he wanted to do well. His photographs would be published as a pictorial article on the latest Italian couture.

As he hung his clothes, he heeded his stomach's call for food, and when finished, he made his way to the second floor dining room and scanned the filled tables. His shoulders sagged, and he realized he shouldn't have wasted time unpacking. The airplane meal had been tedious at best — the typical thimbles of tasteless food. With an appointment in little more than an hour, he felt anxiety rise.

When the maître d' approached and explained he'd have to wait, Paul thought of tipping the man for a reserved seat he guessed was somewhere, but he stopped himself. He needed to ask God's forgiveness for his impatience as much as for his manipulation.

Paul scanned the crowd again, hoping to find someone ready to leave. Instead, his pulse quickened when he spotted his taxi partner. "I know that woman," he said. Before the maître d' could stop him, Paul hurried into the dining room.

As he approached her table, he saw surprise, then irritation, settle on her face. "Do you mind?" he asked, pulling out the chair. "I have an appointment in an hour, and I'm starving."

"You seem to have a lot of emergencies," she said, giving him a restrained nod.

He sank into the chair, wishing he'd made a better first impression. He found her interesting for some unknown reason. Before Paul could apologize, the waiter hurried over and stood while he scanned the menu, made a selection, and placed his order. When the waiter left, Paul folded his hands and gathered his thoughts. "I'm sorry. I've been rather impudent."

"Yes. You have, but thanks for the apology."

"I'm Paul DiAngelo from New York."

Her forehead wrinkled as a flush mottled her cheeks. "From New York?"

He nodded.

"Me, too. I have an apartment in Manhattan."

"I have a place in Jersey City," he said. "I drive through the Holland Tunnel, and I'm in Manhattan."

"Quite a coincidence," she said, extending her hand. "I'm Steffi Rosetti."

"You're Italian, then? Do you have family here?" He saw her wince, leaving him puzzled.

"I'm here for my magazine," she said. "I'm doing a feature article on the Milan Week fashion openings for *Mode*."

For *Mode*? Her statement took the wind out of him. He eyed her sweatshirt, trying to find his breath. "You're kidding," he said finally, motivated by both her attire and the coincidence. "I just hired on with *Mode*. I'm doing a pictorial feature on Milan's fashion week."

Steffi's mouth gaped a moment before she clamped her jaw. She studied his face and, finally, shook her head. "I took you for some kind of seasoned traveler in your sport coat and slacks. You don't dress like any photographer I know."

He shrugged, embarrassed that she caught him in his charade. "I like to dress well."

Her gaze fell to her own garb, then took

24

a slow trip upward to his face. "You can see, I don't worry much about clothes."

Paul wanted to say she should, but he bit back his words. He'd already made a bad impression, and being a fellow co-worker, he needed to mend his ways.

"So where are you off to in such a hurry?" she asked.

Paul was pleased she'd changed the subject. "I have a press conference in" — he eyed his wristwatch — "forty minutes."

"No one let me know about a press conference," she said, obviously annoyed.

The waiter appeared with their meals, and he halted his response. The man refilled their water goblets, then hurried away.

"Come along with me," he said. He managed to keep his gaze from shifting to her unkempt appearance.

"Looking like this? Do you think?" She tugged at her sweatshirt.

Honesty or politeness? He decided to go for honesty. "If you hurry, you can toss on something else."

She jammed her fork into the salad. "I suppose . . . if you think it's necessary."

He swallowed his answer and gazed at his food while his appetite drifted away.

With little conversation, they hurried

their meal, signed the bill, and rushed off in the directions of their rooms with the agreement to meet in ten minutes.

When Paul returned to the lobby, he paced near the doorway, eyeing his watch and expecting her to be late. On the dot, Steffi stepped from the elevator, surprising him. Though she didn't look the picture of fashion, she had made an amazing improvement in her appearance. She wore a long purple sweater over black knit pants. She'd let down her hair — waves of long dark brown tresses — that took his breath away. Over her shoulder, she carried a large tote, her handbag, and a camera. A camera? He swallowed the question, not wanting to ask.

She hurried toward him, and for the first time, she smiled. Her face lit the room.

"Ready?" he asked.

She didn't answer but jiggled the tote and moved toward the door.

He followed, and they stepped outside into the warm spring air. Paul waved his hand at a passing taxi. "We could walk there, but we don't have time, I'm afraid."

A cab pulled up to the curb, and Paul motioned Steffi inside. "Piazza Meda. Starhotel Rosa," Paul said, climbing in beside her. He slammed the door as the driver pulled away. "The press conference is close to the Duomo, the main cathedral in Milan. It's magnificent."

"I'd love to see it . . . to sightsee for that matter," she said, her attention focused on the passing scenery.

Paul watched her out of the corner of his eye. In the hotel lobby, her smile had been fleeting, and now it had vanished. Her full lips pressed together as if in serious thought. He wondered why someone so young — he guessed in her mid-twenties — gave an air of someone weighted with concerns.

"Have you been on foreign assignments before?" he asked.

She kept her head turned, as if not hearing him. Finally, she glanced his way before turning away again. "Mexico City once. I've worked designer openings stateside most of the time."

"I came to Milan once, but as an assistant. I even speak a little Italian."

She gave him another glance. "I heard."

Her voice held a sarcastic note, and he cringed, remembering his obnoxious conversation with the taxi attendant at the airport.

"I hope you can forgive me for that," he said. "Could we start over again?"

He heard her chuckle.

"Why not?" she asked. "I have to thank you for dragging me along on this press conference."

Paul appreciated her willingness to overlook his past behavior. "You're welcome." But as he looked at her, his mind tangled in her long wavy hair and her moody ways. "I like having the company."

He watched the sunlight flicker across her features — her sculptured nose with a hint of freckles and her wide-set eyes as deep blue as the Mediterranean — and could envision her in his camera lens . . . if she would allow it. Still, it wasn't her beauty that caught his attention. Something about her grabbed his heart. Something deep weighed on her soul, and he prayed he could make a difference in her life and be a friend.

Chapter 2

Steffi slid her notebook into her tote bag along with her camera and waited for Paul to pack up his gear. She watched him, remembering their awful meeting, but pleased that she'd had a chance to learn a little more about the man. She had to admit he was generous. He'd invited her to join him at the press conference, and the experience of hearing the couturiers talk about the new fashion trends would give her a head start when she covered the upcoming openings.

In the hotel's large reception room, Steffi stood near the door, hoping Paul would be ready soon. She liked Paul's good looks, the way a sport coat looked just right over his knit shirt. His dark brown hair with a soft wave was parted on the right and had been cut short with a neat sideburn. Not too short. Just right, Steffi thought. She guessed him to be near thirty. His deep laugh lines were punctuated by deep dimples. She'd noticed his dark brown eyes always seemed to hold a smile — except when he was pacing. Then his brow furrowed and he hunched over like an old man. If she got to know him well enough, she would mention that patience is a virtue.

Who was she to tell him anything? She'd been muddling along with problems of her own, not impatience but other flaws that a Christian shouldn't have. She let her mind slip into a prayer that God would uplift her and give her courage to face the challenge of her trip to Italy. Before she'd finished her talk with God, Paul's voice pierced her solitude.

"How'd it go?" he asked.

She drew her mind from her prayer with a quick amen and focused.

"I'm sorry," he said. "I interrupted your thoughts."

She shook her head and hoisted the tote back on her shoulder, avoiding the issue of her musing. "Can we walk back to the hotel?"

"Great idea. Can I carry that for you?" He gestured toward her tote bag.

"I'm fine," she said, struck by the realization that she wasn't fine at all. She needed to think . . . to plan whether or not she would visit her grandmother.

They followed the Via Pattari, and ahead, Steffi could see the magnificent gothic cathedral, its ornate spires, one after another, circling the building. When they reached the Piazza Duomo, she stood back, amazed at the size and beauty of the white marble structure. As she neared, she noticed, amid the spires, statues embedded in the ornate marble design along with gargoyles that hid the rain gutters.

Paul didn't seem to mind the delay as she gazed at the sight. He had delved into his camera bag and had begun to snap pictures from various angles, his lens expanding and retracting, as he changed settings. At times, Steffi sensed he had included her in the photo. She felt like a child, enthralled by the mass of people, the abundance of pigeons, and the many balloon men who hawked their wares to the tourists. She joined Paul, focusing and clicking the lens.

"Can we go inside?" she asked, when Paul drew closer.

He swung his arm, motioning her forward, and she hurried ahead, passing through the wide arched door. Inside, she stood in the darkness until her eyes adjusted from the bright sunlight outside. Awed by the murals and religious statues, Steffi moved into a pew and sat. Paul made his way ahead, stopping to lift his camera to his eye.

In the hush of the cathedral, Steffi let her mind return to her problem. She deliberated the letter from her grandmother — the woman's quest to meet her and comments about her father, a man she didn't remember and who only lived in her memory from her mother's bitter words. *Lord, guide me. Help me find compassion for the grandmother I don't know. Help me make a decision that's pleasing to You. Let it be Your will not mine.*

She lifted her eyes in time to see Paul flagging her toward the door. She eyed her wristwatch in the gloomy light and realized she'd been without sleep for more than twenty-four hours. Rest is what she needed . . . and God's guidance.

Paul sat at the breakfast table alone. He'd invited Steffi to join him, but she wasn't ready, and he disliked waiting for people. He tapped his fingers against the tablecloth, stretching his neck to catch the waiter for a refill on coffee. As he looked, Steffi came into the hotel dining room, and he beckoned to her.

She lifted her hand, letting him know she'd seen him, and headed his way. Today her hair was bound back from her face, her ponytail swinging in rhythm to her steps.

She wore cords and a red sweater that could have held two people, with a hem that hung to her knees. He wondered why she hid beneath such baggy clothes.

He rose, but she yanked out the chair and plopped down, dropping her tote bag beside her on the floor. "What's good?" she asked, picking up the menu and reviewing the options.

"I had the buffet," he said, studying her sullen face and brooding eyes.

She pivoted her head and peered at the selection of food spread over the long table — baskets of rolls and pastries, yogurt, cereals, fresh fruit. She closed the menu and slapped it on the table. "Me, too." She rose, and he watched her move to the buffet to make her selections.

The waiter finally arrived and refilled the coffee. Paul took a sip and pondered Steffi. She filled him with curiosity. He had so many questions that wanted answering. For one, why did she carry her camera? For sightseeing, yes. That made sense. But she took photographs at the press conference. Seeing her juggle her notebook and camera to take pictures irked him. Photography was his job.

Steffi returned, her plate filled with fruit and a container of yogurt. She positioned her breakfast on the table, settled into the chair and, for the first time, focused on him. "What are your plans for today?" She forked a piece of melon and lifted it to her mouth.

His mind thought *to get to know you better,* but he knew not to say it. "Walk around. Take a look at the quadrangle."

She lowered the fork and her brow furrowed. "What's the quadrangle?"

"The fashion quadrangle. The four streets that create a square of Italian designer shops that took the wind out of Paris fashion. Want to come along?"

"Sure. I'd like that."

He liked it, too. Walking and talking was a good way to get to know her better . . . and perhaps understand the reason for the darkness in Steffi's eyes.

The March breeze brushed against Steffi's cheeks as she walked beside Paul. She'd been irritated earlier when he invited her to breakfast and then couldn't wait for her to get ready. But he'd asked her to join him on the walk, and she guessed that made up for it. Her sense of direction was not always perfect . . . though she hated to admit it, and taxis left something to be desired when trying to get the feel for a city.

"Tomorrow's the Armani showing. I'm excited," Steffi said. "I've done so many stateside shows in New York and other locales, but this is different. I'm honored they trusted me enough to do full coverage of Milan's fashion week."

"You must be good," Paul said, giving her a wink.

She shrugged, wondering herself why they'd chosen her to come. She'd worked hard and devoted herself to a project, but she didn't really think she was a great writer.

"What's that?" she asked, approaching a large arch over the street in front of her. Its multi-toned blocks of gray stone looked like a bulwark.

"I think it's the Porta Nuova. It closes the street. Some historical event, I've heard, but when we pass beyond it, the street name changes to Manzoni. That's where the fashion district begins."

They passed beneath the arch and, after a couple of blocks, turned onto Via della Spiga. Wending their way through the streets, they paused to look inside the boutiques, the shelves nearly bare, the counters polished wood and glass as sparkling as diamonds. Top designer names flashed past their eyes, and in the unique window lighting, Paul caught reflections of Steffi — her pouting mouth, her dark lashes that canopied amazing eyes that reflected a troubled soul.

He couldn't resist and lifted his camera lens to focus on her pensive face.

When she noticed him, she held up her hands. "Don't photograph me. Here," she said, dropping her tote to the ground and tugging out her camera, "let me take you."

He laughed and posed like a male model beside a shop window, blackened glass leaving only an oval of clear, like a cameo that framed one pair of leather shoes and matching handbag. Such opulence, he'd never seen in the States.

His curiosity got the best of him as they turned the corner and moved along Via Sant Andrea. "Why do take your own photographs at events? That's my job."

She shrugged.

"Do you think I should take notes in case you don't do your job?"

"That's different," she said, turning away and gazing into the windows.

He didn't think it was, but why argue? The situation was a trust factor. Trust. Was that an issue for Steffi? His spirit sagged. Perhaps trust was a clue to her problems. He thanked God for the small hint. One day maybe Steffi would trust him enough to open the door of her heart and let him in.

On Sunday afternoon, Steffi experienced her first opening. The Armani unveiling dazzled the crowd with slim jackets, column dresses, and soft leather pencil skirts. The color palette was a blend of gray and beige with splashes of richer hues used as accents. Steffi gawked at the famous personalities and wealthy citizens who sat in narrow rows along the catwalk, but she kept control of her excitement, knowing her role as a journalist and hoping to appear professional and unaffected by the glamour that surrounded her. Funny. She wouldn't be caught dead in one of the garments she saw. Steffi liked her loose slacks and oversized tops. In a way, they kept her safe from many of life's ills.

Steffi wrestled with balancing her notebook while adjusting her camera. Paul's question came to mind — why did she take her own photos? To make sure, would have been her answer. She hurt his feelings, she suspected, remembering his comment about writing her story. She lifted the camera and followed the supermodel who strutted along the walkway, looking as if she hadn't eaten since the previous year.

Across the floor, Paul had settled into the perfect vantage point. She watched him when she had time to shift her attention from the notepad, admiring his concentration in the midst of madness. She'd admired him a day earlier at the press conference when she'd been jostled by a taller journalist. Paul had stepped in with tact and spoken to the gentleman. In a flash, the man apologized and made room for Steffi in her rightful place in a press area. She'd seen Paul's generous side so often, but yesterday he'd shown integrity. What he still hadn't revealed was patience.

The show ended in a burst of applause, followed by the hum of conversation. Steffi dropped her notes into her shoulder tote, then headed toward the door. Paul caught up with her, his camera still hanging around his neck. His shirttail had pulled out, and she grinned, happy to see him, for once, not his usual vision of neatness.

"What's the smile for?" he asked.

"You . . . and your shirttail."

He glanced down and gave it a quick tuck before eyeing her. "I've been meaning to talk to you about that."

"About what? Shirttails?"

Paul chuckled and took her arm as they stepped into the night air. "No, about your choice of attire."

She stiffened with his comment. "What's wrong with my attire?"

"Nothing, if you . . ." He shrugged. "Nothing." His voice lost its good humor.

"If I didn't look like I'd just climbed off a tractor?" She arched a purposeful eyebrow.

At that, he laughed. "Something like that."

"I like how I dress."

He didn't respond, and she ambled alongside him, wondering what he was thinking. She'd expected a comeback. She heard none.

"Ready to head back?" Paul asked.

"I'd like to walk for awhile. You can go on ahead." She sidled a glance, hoping he would walk with her.

"I won't leave you alone," he said. "It's a nice day. Let's walk back."

Steffi's mind filled with questions. She wanted to know why Paul cared how she looked. Didn't he know the most important part of a human was what was inside? Her mother had said that her father had been a handsome man. Dashing, she called him — well-dressed and well-groomed, but that didn't make him beautiful inside, where it counted.

Paul wanted to kick himself for his comment about her clothes. The whole thing was self-serving. She didn't want to look like a supermodel. He wanted her to, but why? The question rattled in his head as they walked along the ancient streets toward the hotel. In the silence, an answer struck him. Because beneath her self-control, he sensed a woman tormented . . . a woman who did not like herself very much.

Another question fell into his mind. Why? How could an apparently talented woman with charm and beauty not have self-worth?

"You're the quiet one this time," she said, her soft voice puncturing his thoughts.

"Just thinking . . . about you." He swallowed the anxiety that rose from his comment. Would she now back away from him?

"About me? Why would you be thinking about me?"

"Loads of things, but right now I was wondering —"

"Why I dress the way I do?"

She'd finished his sentence incorrectly, and he breathed a relieved sigh. Why get into all the other puzzling things about her? "No. I wasn't thinking of that at all."

She didn't ask, and he didn't offer. He wondered how she would react if she knew about the photographs he'd taken of her — shots so lovely they took his breath away. He'd caught her in a blend of light and shadow. Her pensive downturned face tugged at his heart. Paul had been delighted when he realized he'd snapped a shot of a rare smile at the Piazza Duomo. Steffi's face had been upturned to the sun, and behind her a mélange of bright balloons filled the sky.

"I have something to show you when we get back to the hotel," he said, after sending a prayer to God to cover him with blessing.

"What?"

"Just wait . . . but it'll explain why you were on my mind."

She frowned, as if she didn't understand.

"I mean, you'll know why I was thinking of you," he said, answering her unasked question.

Their footsteps tapped along the concrete sidewalk, bouncing off the rococo facade of the building they passed, and at the

Piazza Cavour, instead of turning, they headed up Via Manin, an indirect route to the hotel. They passed the elegant Belgioioso, at one time Napoleon's residence, and headed for the public gardens.

In the park, they ambled past ponds and shrubs, enjoying the spring flowers that blossomed from neat beds.

"It's beautiful," Steffi said, settling on a bench. She opened her tote bag and pulled out her camera, then stood back and focused on Paul.

"No fair," he said, giving her his brightest smile.

She laughed, and the lilt of her voice touched his heart. She should smile more often. He kept the thought to himself.

When she'd finished and turned toward the scenery, he pulled the lens cap off his camera. "My turn."

She swung around, and he brought the lens in close, catching her surprised look as the late afternoon sunlight played upon wisps of hair that had broken loose from their bonds and played against her cheek. When she realized what he'd done, she turned her back.

"I don't like pictures of myself," she said.

His heart sank, knowing he planned to

show her the other photos he'd taken once they returned to the hotel.

Again, he was puzzled. Why did she dislike her picture being taken? She troubled him . . . concerned him. He wanted to know so many things about her.

God willing, he would.

Chapter 3

Steffi sat in the hotel lounge, sipping a soft drink and waiting for Paul, who'd run to his room to bring back the surprise he'd mentioned. She'd tried to guess what it might be, but she had no idea. Paul seemed full of surprises. They'd spent time together, enjoying the city and its history, and even with his limited Italian, he read signs and guided her to the most intriguing places, like today when he took her to the park.

When she looked toward the elevator, the door slid open, and Paul stepped into the lobby. He'd removed his jacket and now looked more casual in a knit shirt the color of milk chocolate, the same color as his eyes. Under his arm, he carried a folder. Awareness hit her. A portfolio. He'd wanted to show her his photographs.

His eyes smiled at her as he sank into the cushion at her side. "I hope you're ready for this."

The comment made her curious, and right away, she assumed he wanted to show her how terrific his pictures were, guessing

44

that hers would not be nearly as good. "Mine aren't developed, yet."

Paul pressed his hand against her arm, keeping the portfolio closed. "I'm not trying to compete, Steffi. I want you to see something special."

His voice sounded tender, and the tone wove through her, wrapping around her heart. She placed the album on her lap and opened the page. She was struck by the exquisite detail, the play of light, the unique tilt of the lens. More than a fashion shoot, these photos were creative.

"Extraordinary," she said, turning the pages. "You have a great eye for exceptional photographs."

"Those aren't the pictures I was referring to," he said.

Paul's tone held a mysterious sound that caused her to turn and look into his eyes. With her gaze riveted to his, she felt him turn numerous pages. Then with the tilt of his head, he spoke. "These are the ones."

Her breath caught as she gaped down at the photographs. She flipped the pages, realizing each shot was her in the Piazza Duomo, in the fashion quadrangle, places she'd never known he'd snapped her pictures. The images amazed her. For the first time, she saw herself as he saw her — her pensive face, her sullen mouth, her rare smile looking into the heavens. She'd never liked her photograph taken, but the pictures intrigued her with the play of sun and shadow.

"You're a beautiful woman," he said, brushing his finger across her arm.

Steffi's chest tightened, hearing his words, and her immediate reaction was to run away from his flattery. He was mocking her, baiting her for something.

"Don't frown, Steffi. I'm only telling you the truth. I have no other agenda . . . than to get to know you better. You drive me crazy. You puzzle me."

"But I . . . I don't understand why you took these."

"I just told you. You're fascinating inside and out."

She felt the gentle caress on her arm, and the warmth traveled upward and nestled near her heart. He'd said he told the truth. Could she believe him? Could she trust him?

"I hope you're not angry. A photographer can't pass up an exceptional subject." He studied her face a moment before continuing. "You don't trust me for some reason. I wish I knew why."

Disappointment washed across his face

like the sun fading behind a cloud. She'd doused his pleasure with her inability to say thank you, her fear to show approval. "They're very nice photographs. You've just surprised me. Thanks for letting me see them."

She placed the portfolio on the table in front of her, then took a sip of the soft drink.

"You're welcome," he said, disappointment reflecting in his voice.

They sat in silence before Paul flagged the waiter and placed his order. When the man had gone, he shifted his hip on the cushion to face her more directly. "Tell me about yourself."

His request sent tendrils of surprise and sadness weaving through her veins. "Why? What do you want to know?"

"Why you're so sad."

The blunt comment punctured her security. "I'm not sad. I'm thoughtful."

"Then why are you so thoughtful?"

Paul watched Steffi's expression shuffle through a myriad of emotion. Part of him grieved that he'd asked the question. Part of him rejoiced that he'd had the courage to speak the words that had lain in his heart since he'd met her.

"I have a lot on my mind, Paul."

"I realize we've just met, but I'm a good listener. What kind of things?"

"I don't want to talk about them." She pulled her gaze away.

Her blunt response whacked his curiosity, but he wanted to keep the door open, and he scuffled for a response. "Okay. Let's talk about me, then. Any questions?"

Her gaze shifted across his face as if trying to figure out if he was serious.

"Anything?" she asked.

"Sure, why not? Try me."

Steffi puffed out her cheeks, releasing a breath before she spoke. "Why are you so impatient? I've never met anyone who paces more or looks at his watch more than you."

She'd struck home with her question. He decided to go for a lighthearted response. "Me? Impatient?"

Her serious expression melted to a grin. "Then what do you call it?"

"Eager. Sensitive."

Her laugh surprised him.

"Really?" Her smile retraced itself to a serious look. "Are you a Christian? I have the feeling you are."

Paul wondered where that question came from. "All my life. I'm not always the

48

best church attender, but God guides my steps." She'd piqued his own interest. "How about you?"

"Same as you," she said. "I believe in the Lord, but I probably don't demonstrate it as I should, and then there're things in my life that . . ."

Paul waited for her to complete the statement, eager to learn a little bit more about her. But she stopped. His mouth felt dry, and his attention shifted to the bar, wondering what had happened to his drink. He checked his wristwatch, and felt distracted for a moment, trying to remember how long it had been since he'd placed his order.

Steffi's silence broke with a chuckle. "I see you're being sensitive."

"Sensitive?"

"Oh, then it must be eager." She tapped her fingernails on the table, rolling them in a grumbling rhythm, as if taunting him.

He got the point. "Yes. I'm . . . *eager* for my drink."

A told-you-so grin curved her mouth, but he didn't give her the pleasure of response. Instead, he caught the waiter's attention and pointed to his empty hand.

The man nodded, and in a moment, he

49

returned with a tumbler of soda. *"Scusi. Per fa ritardore."*

"Grazie," Paul said, taking his drink.

The man left, and Steffi looked at Paul with a frown. "What did he say?"

"He was sorry for the delay."

Steffi nodded. "So let's get back to this impatience thing. You can call it anything you want."

She looked uncomfortable, and Paul wondered what was on her mind.

She tilted her head and gave him a shy look. "If you're a Christian, then you know that God tells us to be patient. 'Clothe yourself with compassion, kindness, humility, gentleness and patience.' It's in Colossians."

"I know that scripture. 'And over all these virtues put on love.' That's my favorite part of the verse." Though he was teasing her on one hand, he truly believed love was what bound people together.

"Get serious. Admit you're probably one of the most impatient people on earth."

"I am being serious. I think without love we're nothing." He watched the same brooding look glaze her eyes. He'd hit home again, and he longed to reach out and touch her . . . to help her through whatever painful experience she had endured.

Yet, knowing better, he decided to talk about himself. Perhaps his example would open the door. "Okay. I admit it. I'm impatient. I don't know why, Steffi. Maybe because I was an only child and so I often got my way. My parents doted on me. I could do no wrong."

Her face paled as he spoke, and he could only assume that her childhood must have been part of the explanation for her sad eyes.

"When I got older, I realized that I could do wrong and I wasn't perfect, but I still liked having things come to me as quickly as they did when I was a kid. Not realistic, but truthful."

She nodded. "Many life expectations aren't realistic."

No expectations. No trust. No hope. Was this her life's motto? If so, he ached for her.

Steffi jumped at the telephone's ring. She wrapped the towel tighter around her wet body and hurried to the telephone. "Hello," she said, eyeing the clock. Another opening would begin in less than an hour, and she was running late.

"Good morning." Paul's pleasant voice sailed across the wire. "Ready? We need to get going."

"I'm not quite ready." She looked down at the white hotel towel and felt her wet hair cling against her back.

"How long?"

She listened for impatience in his voice, but she sensed he was making a valiant effort to control it. "Another fifteen." She knew she was pushing it, but she'd do her best.

"We'll be late. Even if we can catch a cab, the traffic will be horrible there today, and walking will take a good twenty-five minutes. I don't want to be late."

"Don't be so impatient." She grimaced at her ploy.

"I'm not being impatient. I'm being realistic. I can't miss the show and neither can you."

"So go without me." She tried to catch the drips from her hair with the corner of the towel. Her reflection in the mirror made her cringe. She would be late if she didn't fly. "I don't want you to be late."

She lowered the phone, feeling sorry as soon as she heard the click of the receiver on the cradle. He was right. She had to be on time. Flying back into the bathroom, she dried, pulled on her clothes, slid into her shoes, then faced the mirror. The comb slid through her hair with a few tugs to get out the snarls. She'd let it air dry on the way. She sent a praise to God for natural waves. After a daub of lipstick and mascara, Steffi took a final look, grabbed her tote, and ran out the door.

Paul wasn't waiting in the lobby as she'd hoped. Outside, she stood on the corner, trying to flag a cab, but each time they flew past as if she wasn't there. She glanced at her watch, then tugged her street map from her shoulder bag and studied it a moment. The Galleria was near the Duomo. She certainly could find her way. It was straight down Turati, which changed to Manzoni, and she would be almost there.

She struck out at a brisk pace, keeping an eye on her wristwatch. She waited at streetlights, her patience about as short as Paul's. As she passed La Scala, the famous opera house with its arched overhang to protect the carriages which brought the patrons centuries earlier, she saw the spires of the Duomo and the glass dome of the Galleria. Having nearly run the stretch from the hotel, she had arrived with five minutes to spare. The crowd jostled outside the building, but she paused a moment to watch the sunlight glint from the glass rooftop. It was one of those photo opportunities that Paul had mentioned.

She shuffled through her tote and pulled out her camera, focusing on the diamond glints that shimmered from the roof. She pushed the shutter release, hoping the photograph would capture the loveliness she'd witnessed. Hearing the rewinding buzz, Steffi realized she'd used her last picture. Frustrated at her lack of planning, she shoved her arm into her bag and pulled out a fresh roll of film.

"Signorina needs help?"

She looked up to see a nicely dressed gentleman standing beside her. "Thanks. I have to load my camera." She finagled trying to hold the camera while removing the film from the box.

"Let me help," he said, taking the camera from her hands.

She gave him a nod and, with two hands, removed the film from its housing. When she looked up, she saw the man's back running away . . . with her camera. Frustration at her own stupidity filled her mind. "Stop him," she yelled, remembering how many times she'd been told to watch out for pickpockets, and she'd fallen prey.

The man vanished in the bustling crowd, people heading for the opening and others toward the Piazza Duomo. Her shoulders sagged as she dropped the useless film into her tote. She didn't even have time to find a policeman.

She moved through the wide arched entrance into the street arcade. A glass ceiling with a central dome covered the way between Piazza La Scala and the cathedral. She made her way to the center where the temporary stage and catwalk had been constructed. The chairs lining the walkway were already filled with people, and the press area was crowded with journalists.

Steffi elbowed her way through the crowd, tears in her eyes from the loss of her camera and her own stupidity for not listening to the warnings she'd heard over and over. When she spotted Paul, her control left her, and tears rolled down her cheeks as quickly as she could brush them away with the back of her hand.

"What happened?" he said, his gaze shifting from her to the catwalk. She realized he didn't want to miss the show's beginning.

His voice could barely be heard above the music that reverberated from the ornate walls of the buildings that lined each side of the street and from the colorful mosaic tiled floor. "A pickpocket stole my camera."

Paul's eyes widened, and he leaned closer. "Stole your camera?"

With her throat knotted with emotion, she could only nod.

"I'm sorry, Steffi," he said, wrapping his arm around her shoulders and drawing her to him. He leaned closer to her ear. "Did you report it to the police?"

With her head buried in his chest, she only shook her head.

"We will later . . . after the show."

She knew she would never see her camera again, but she appreciated his effort to soothe her.

He lifted a hand and tilted her chin upward. She met his gaze, and a flutter in her chest made her breathless.

"I won't let you travel around here alone anymore," he said. "I'm sorry I left ahead of you."

"It was my fault," she whispered, as the music's pounding rhythm warned them the show was to begin.

"Let's not talk about fault," he said in her ear. "Let's talk about sticking together."

Chapter 4

Paul pulled out a chair and Steffi sank into it. He helped her scoot forward, then rounded the table and joined her. Frustration at himself and her permeated his thoughts. Why had he let her find her own way to the Galleria? Why had she been so unthinking to let a stranger hold her camera?

"Thanks for talking with the police," Steffi said, opening the menu and staring at the selections. "I know it's useless, but I appreciate the valiant effort."

"You never know." He agreed that it was hopeless, but at least he'd tried. "Why did you have your camera out anyway?"

Steffi told him the story of the Galleria roof and running out of film. She also relayed her inability to flag a cab. "I have to be honest with you. I wasn't at all ready when you called, and if you'd hung around I probably would have dawdled. I hurried, hoping to catch up with you in the lobby."

"Thanks for trusting me enough to tell me the truth." Her openness seemed one step closer to her confiding in him. If she didn't, how could he help her?

"I'd just gotten out of the shower. I was wet and my hair was sopped."

He grinned. "Next time, we'll both do better."

Her eyes searched his, then she smiled.

She refocused on the menu, and he did the same. They each selected a pasta, and once the waiter left, Paul took a drink of water and spoke the words he hated to say. "The fashion week ends in a couple days. Then, it's back to New York for you."

Steffi shrugged. "I'm not sure. I have another week. I might stay on."

"Really? I've taken vacation time, too. I figured, how often will I get a free trip to Italy? I might take a couple of side trips before going home."

Though she'd focused on him, he observed the faraway look in her eyes.

"Will you stay in Milan?" Paul asked. She needed to talk. It was obvious. *Lord, if You would only open the door to her heart, and let me in.*

"I'm thinking of . . . Venice."

Her voice had lost its momentum. "Venice. I've never been there, but I'd love to go. The Grand Canal, St. Mark's Square, Doges Palace. I've only seen photographs."

"Me, too." She kept her eyes focused on her water glass, her finger running along the edge.

He watched the unending trips her finger made around the rim, going nowhere . . . like Steffi's troubles. "There's more to it than that. I know you too well now."

Her hand continued to trace the circle, but it finally slowed, and she looked up. "Yes. There's more."

This time he knew better than to say *tell me*. She needed to make the decision for herself. Fighting the desire to ask questions and probe, he captured her gaze and waited. If Steffi ever recognized patience, it was now.

Silence hovered over the table until she released a ragged sigh. "It's a long story," she said.

He looked at his watch, then gave her a heartfelt grin. "We have all the time in the world."

Paul's patience paid off, and his hopes rose as Steffi began the story of her father's abandonment, her mother's bitterness, and the sorrow she'd felt throughout her life.

"I missed having a father," she said. "Now that I'm an adult it's not as important, but years ago, I felt to blame. He left

59

after I was born. I was two years old. I figured he didn't want a child, or maybe, I was too whiny for his liking."

"Steffi." Paul shook his head, amazed she would think that way. "Hadn't you realized a two year old couldn't break up a marriage? Only teenagers can do that." He gave her a playful smile, trying to lighten the heavy conversation.

She grinned back, but her eyes didn't smile. "Kids don't think logically. Once rejected, it's hard to open up again."

Enlightened, Paul grasped the thought. "It's difficult to trust and to have expectations."

She nodded. "That's right. And my mother didn't help the situation, but I don't want to blame her. She was as hurt as I was. Worse, I'm sure."

Paul could only imagine. He'd come from a stable home with two loving parents. How might his life have changed if a divorce had occurred? He couldn't imagine it. "So your parents divorced?"

"No."

He gaped at her, his mind swirling with bewilderment. "You mean they remained married all those years?"

She seemed as puzzled as he was. "Yes. My father returned to Italy, my mother told me, and we never heard from him again. Mom never divorced him. I don't know why. Maybe religious reasons. Maybe not. She won't talk about it."

The information confounded him, and he could only imagine how it would be to spend your life without answers to probing questions. "So that's it, then." He reached across the table and touched her hand. The feeling seemed so right. Baggy shirts and jeans? Paul didn't care. Steffi was beautiful in his eyes from inside out. "You'll never know what really happened."

She closed her eyes, and he could see tears rim her lashes.

"What is it?" he asked. "What's wrong?"

She turned away and delved into her shoulder bag, sitting between her feet. When she lifted her hand above the table, she brought up a crumpled envelope. "Here. Read this."

Confused and concerned, he pressed the creases from the jacket and pulled out cream-colored stationery, trimmed with a black border. The black tugged at his remembrance. In European countries, the black borders stood for death. Paul unfolded the letter, then thought better of it. "Are you sure you want me to read this?"

"I'm positive. I need advice . . . and a friend."

Her words lifted his spirit and tangled around his heart. He'd longed since he met her to hear Steffi say those words. He scanned the letter, emotion skittering through him as he read the plaintive words of the grandmother. When he finished, he lifted his eyes to hers. "What kind of advice do you need?" He prayed it wasn't what he feared.

"Should I go?"

Paul had been right. How could she not go to visit this woman who'd opened her heart? "Do you have a choice?" He searched her face, hoping to see a flicker of an answer. "She's your grandmother."

She lowered her head, and before she lifted it, the waiter arrived with their meals. Paul thanked him and when he'd gone, he asked again, "Do you have a choice?"

Her eyes downcast, she released a deep sigh. "I could ignore the letter like my father did us twenty-three years ago."

Paul reached forward and clasped her hands in his. "Could you really do that?"

When Steffi lifted her gaze, tears filled her eyes. "I don't think so, but . . ."

"But it's difficult. I agree with you." Paul didn't release her hand, but held it captive.

"I think what you have to keep in the forefront is that this woman" — he touched the letter — "isn't the one who left you years ago. She wanted to get in touch, but your father told her to stay out of his business. He had his reasons, Steffi. You'll only learn why when you go to see her."

She didn't respond, but he saw in her face the struggle that tormented her thoughts.

He gave her hand a squeeze. "Let's talk about this tomorrow. Work through your thoughts and tell me tomorrow what you're thinking. I want to help you."

Steffi agreed, and they both faced their plates, their appetites diminished by the tension that had wrought them for the past minutes.

"Dig in," he said, sending her a silly smile.

She laughed, and the lilt warmed him. He saw hope in her eyes. He would pray tonight that the good Lord would help her find the answer.

"Two more openings," she released a puff of air from her lungs. "This is hard work. I've spent all my free time writing up my notes and trying to get them into the laptop. I've been sending reviews of the openings each night, but now they tell me they want a feature article on the full event."

Paul rested his back against the lounge chair and sipped his soft drink. "I wonder if they've changed their minds. Maybe they're using my photography to illustrate your article."

"They didn't say. Could be."

He frowned and rubbed his chin. "I'm not sure I like that. They sent me here for a pictorial feature. I'd hate —"

Steffi pressed her hand on his arm. "I'm sure it will be what they assigned. They may include a full fashion week review in the same issue." She felt her eyebrows lift, asking without saying the words. She'd never seen Paul appear so sensitive and unsure about his work. He'd always had an air of confidence.

"I suppose you're right. I sound like a spoiled kid."

Not spoiled in her eyes, perhaps more humble than she realized. He seemed to doubt his ability, and that surprised her. No matter what his flaws, she liked him anyway. She liked him a lot. Steffi sipped her coffee, getting her thoughts around the words she planned to say. The dark brew rolled on her tongue and warmed her throat. "I've made a decision."

His head lifted with the speed of a lightning bolt. He didn't ask. He reached over and took her hand. She loved the feel of closeness — a feeling she had avoided most of her life for fear of being hurt, of being forsaken by someone who meant too much to her.

"I'm going to Venice, but . . . I'll have to find the courage to visit her. I might just call."

"Oh . . . Steffi, I —" He shook his head. "It's not my business. You do what you must, but here's a thought. Let me go with you. I have the time, and I've never seen Venice. That's not a place to go alone."

"It's not?" She thought of the pickpocket who stole her camera. "You mean it's —"

"Venice is the city of love. Amore." He flashed her a heartwarming smile. "You can't be alone in a town like that."

His look sent a ripple through her chest. Paul had shown compassion for her, and it soothed her. He'd reached out to her and touched her life with his funny world of impatience — although she had to admit he was making an effort to improve — and optimism. She needed someone who could help her see the bright side of life. She'd asked the Lord for direction, but Steffi realized she didn't listen well to God's guidance. Steffi struggled along on her own until all else failed, then she turned to the Lord's bidding. When would she learn?

"I can't ask you to come with me. I'm too depressing."

He laughed. "And I'm the guy who can make you smile. You need me."

She did smile at his silliness. "I suppose it wouldn't hurt. You could help me find my way and then —"

"Then I'll leave you be. You need to visit your grandmother on your own, but I'll support you. Yes." His countenance brightened like the glinting roof she'd admired on the Galleria.

"Let's celebrate," he said. "We have another show today, and the final opening. Tomorrow night we could find a wonderful restaurant . . . a really special place to have dinner to enjoy our last night in Milan."

Steffi's stomach twisted with the truth. "I can't."

"You can't? But why?" His face faded from bright to dim.

She tugged at her sweater. "I have no clothes for a nice restaurant."

"Hmm?" he rubbed his chin as if in thought.

Steffi realized he was teasing her, but she waited.

"Let's see. We're in Milan, fashion capital of Italy. Perhaps we could find a shop where you could buy some new clothes."

"I couldn't touch the price with my whole savings." She shook her head, knowing that was the truth.

"Have you heard of designer outlets? Just like our shops at home. Exclusive stores that sell at a discount. What do you say?"

His eyes glowed with excitement, and she hated to disappoint him. Clothes were not her friends. She liked comfort, not style. He should know that by now. "We could eat at the fast food restaurant at the Galleria. The building's lovely." She gave him a feeble smile.

He grinned back but lifted his shoulders in defeat, then rallied. "Do you remember those photos I took, Steffi? Did you see your face? Your hair? You're so pretty, but you hide it all beneath those baggy things you wear."

She shrugged, hoping to dissuade him from talking about her looks. She'd worn dowdy clothes all her life to avoid relationships. He was trying to undermine her tactic.

"I understand now," he said. "You want to avoid getting attached to people so you make yourself as unattractive as possible, but you see it didn't work. You know why?"

She didn't, and she feared he would tell her something about herself that she didn't even know. She shook her head.

"Because anyone of worth looks inside first. When they find the beauty inside, the outside doesn't matter. In your case, Steffi, you're lovely inside and out."

Tears pressed behind her eyes, and she lowered her head so other diners wouldn't see her emotion. He'd called her beautiful . . . inside. She never thought of herself as beautiful in any way, even though people often told her she was attractive — although they usually added, "If you'd fix yourself up."

He covered her hand with his. "I'm not trying to upset you. You want me to be truthful, and I am."

"Thank you," she whispered.

When she raised her head, she saw his eyes filled with concern.

"I'm fine," she said. "You just surprised me with your comments."

"You shouldn't be surprised, Steffi. People should have told you how good you are all along. Good to the depth of your being, not just surface . . . although that's nice to hear, too."

He lifted her hand and pressed it between his. "It's time you let your beauty shine. You want your grandmother to see the best side of you, don't you? Whether it gives credit to your mother or your father, she needs to see the real you."

His words settled into her thoughts. *The real you.* Did she really know who she was? Sometimes she wondered. Her life had been a blend of disappointment and bewilderment, of grief and bitterness. She wondered how Paul could see that she had beauty from within. He had made a good point, though. If . . . and that was *if* she went to see her grandmother, she might as well present herself in the best light possible. No matter what had happened in the past, she wanted her grandmother to know that her mother had raised her well. Her mother had raised her to be a Christian despite her bitterness, and that was a gift in itself.

Chapter 5

Paul grabbed Steffi's hand and urged her into the intriguing shopping mall. Like a little Italian city, the shops stood behind arcades with covered walkways spanning the shops a story above the street. A large cupola rose above the roof, and as Paul tilted his head to see the dome, he noticed the wrought iron balconies that extended from the second-story shops.

"It's charming," Steffi said, craning her neck to catch all the sights. Designer names adorned the windows of the shops selling famous couture discounted up to seventy percent.

With Steffi's hand still in his, Paul drew her into a nearby shop. Though she resisted, she moved ahead, gazing at the price tags and lifting her eyebrows to announce the prices were still too exorbitant. As Paul wandered among the displays, he handed Steffi one garment after another, prodding her to give it a try.

Finally, she grudgingly headed into a dressing room. He sank into a chair and waited, confident he would be there awhile, but to his surprise, Steffi came through the doorway in a heartbeat. She wore a skirt and top that seemed meant for her. The black leather skirt nestled against her shapely frame, and the ruby-red knit top curved beneath her neck and swept down her arms, a perfect fit.

"Looks good," he said, giving her a thumbs up. But she looked more than good. She looked better than any supermodel he'd seen on the catwalk.

"If I buy this, I'll need boots." She lifted her foot and pointed to her made-for-comfort walking shoes.

"So?"

She shrugged and hurried back inside. In a moment, Steffi returned with the same skirt, but a different top, a silky blouse in black and teal shades, perfect for her dark coloring.

He sent her a wink. "I like it."

When they made the purchases, they moved on and visited store after store, wandering through the displays and weighing the value of one item over another. Steffi's taste in attire astounded him. She put together skirts with sweaters and vests that looked made for each other. He wondered how she could know so much about fashion and still wear those baggy clothes. Then he recalled their conversation and remembered her unorthodox appearance was part of her defense.

Today he rejoiced that she'd let down her guard, trusting him enough to add some new items to her wardrobe . . . for her grandmother and, just perhaps, for his admiring look.

Before they left, Steffi had added black stylish boots, a dress that sent his heart on a whirl, and more garments than he could recall. Paul had made two purchases — a new designer shirt for himself and a cashmere sport coat, but the best was a surprise for Steffi. He'd had one opportunity to steal away while she was preoccupied, and after purchasing the gift, he dropped the package into the other shopping bag so she wouldn't see the store logo.

Exhausted, they returned to the hotel, and in his room, Paul realized he needed to make reservations at Il Teatro. The restaurant was well known and in the fashion quadrangle. The setting seemed an appropriate place to celebrate their last night in Milan.

When Paul hung up the telephone, he leaned back in the lone chair in his room. He eyed the gift he would give Steffi before dinner when he went to her room to escort her to the restaurant. To him, the evening seemed their first official date, and he knew a gentleman always picked up the woman at her home.

He smiled to himself, thinking of the happiness he'd felt the past week with Steffi in his company. Their unpleasant meeting had faded in his memory, and he was grateful. She'd been kind to forgive him, and he prayed the Lord had done the same. He'd acted pompous and rude. With the Lord in his thoughts, Paul slid his Bible from the table beside him. He opened the pages and let his eyes rest on God's Word.

With all that had passed, Paul sensed in his heart that the Lord was at work in his life. In New York, he'd allowed his social life to become mundane. Nothing excited him except his work. No woman had caught his eye, and as far as he had been concerned, he didn't need anyone. But since he'd arrived, he'd learned something new. He didn't need anyone. Instead, he yearned for someone with whom to enjoy life. He remembered a Bible verse from Ecclesiastes that said something about two people are better than one. He'd begun to feel the same.

Two are better. Like Noah and the ark, two were company, two were support, two were partners in life's joys and trials. He wanted to wipe away Steffi's tears and give her the love she'd avoided for so long. Paul sensed the Lord had brought their paths together for that purpose. *And over all these virtues put on love, which binds them all together in perfect unity.* The scripture summarized the deep feeling that had been growing in his heart.

Cautioning himself, Paul closed his eyes, realizing he'd only known Steffi a week, but in that week, he'd given more and accepted more than he had in years. Since he and Steffi worked together at *Mode*, he knew that God was offering them time for their relationship to grow. With confidence, Paul accepted the thought.

He could only hope that Steffi would someday feel the same.

Steffi slid her hands beneath her hair and clasped the delicate choker she'd found in the hotel's boutique. A chain of black beads between rows of gold links looked perfect with the new dress she'd purchased. Paul had admired the gown, and though she'd never dreamed she would wear something so lovely, she'd tried it on and agreed. The black lace bodice and sheath skirt veiled a shimmering deep rose lining. The material slid over her like gossamer threads, making her feel special.

Paul had been good for her. He'd brought out her best qualities that had lain deep inside her, afraid to come to the surface for fear of rejection. When she thought of going back to New York, sadness filled her — not that she wouldn't see Paul again, but that life would get in the way and they would drift apart.

Steffi slipped on the black-strapped pumps she'd brought from home, a last-minute decision, and took a final look. She liked what she saw. When she turned away from the mirror, she heard a rap on the door. Her heart jigged through her chest, and she grinned at the silliness of her emotions. The caller was only Paul. But as she thought the words, she knew she was fooling herself. He'd come to mean so much to her.

She peeked through the hole and seeing his face, Steffi pulled open the door.

Paul's eyes widened and he gave her a slow whistle. "Where have you been all my life?"

He stepped inside and took a quick look

at the room before returning to her. "You look lovely."

"Thank you," she said, wanting to press her hand against her chest to hold back the intense beat of her heart.

"Your room looks exactly like mine. Big surprise." He flashed her a grin and held up a package. "I didn't bring a corsage, but I have a present for you."

She looked at the package, wondering if she'd heard him correctly. "A present?"

"You know . . . a gift." He extended the tissue-covered item.

She shook her head. "When did you buy me a gift . . . and why?"

"Because I like you, and I bought it when you weren't looking."

She chuckled. "Obviously." She sat on the corner of the bed and pulled off the wrapping. When she saw the gift, tears welled in her eyes. "Paul, you shouldn't have." She studied the new camera, so much better than the one she'd owned. "You didn't have to do this."

"How can you take photos of your grandmother without a camera?"

His tender look took her breath away. "What can I say?" She placed the camera on the spread and rose, placing her arms around his neck. She drew him into an embrace, loving the feel of him in her arms and lost in the spicy scent of his aftershave.

He held her tight, and when she eased back to look in his eyes, she couldn't move. His gentle face said so much more than words. His gaze lowered to her mouth, and he moved forward, his lips brushing hers so sweetly, her knees weakened.

"You're welcome," he said, holding her in his embrace. "I thought you'd like it."

His kiss had flustered her and thrilled her at the same time. She opened her mouth to speak and found her wits had taken a vacation. Finally, her senses returned. "I more than like it. I love it."

"I'm glad. I wish I could give you everything your heart desires."

His words touched her deeply.

"Are you ready?" he asked.

She grabbed her black wrap and followed him through the door.

As Paul organized his gear for a final shoot, he could not forget the previous evening. Steffi dressed in a shimmer of black and a rich flowery pink hidden beneath the lace. Her hair had fallen around her shoulders in a billow of waves, her dark blue eyes looking at him with trust in one of those wonderful moments. He'd taken a chance and kissed her. The gamble had been worthwhile. She'd accepted his lips and his embrace beyond his expectation.

The restaurant had been as perfect as he'd imagined. Lodged inside the Four Seasons Hotel, the area was surrounded by columns and frescos from a fifteenth century cloister. Inside, Steffi's eyes widened as she gazed at the murals, lavish bouquets of fresh flowers, and the porcelain and brass decor. The tables were covered with white linen and set with elegant china and crystal stemware. Paul had paid a handsome sum, but seeing the wonder in Steffi's eyes made the cost worthwhile.

Today, Paul faced his final couture opening. Taking one final review of his equipment, he picked up the receiver and punched in Steffi's number. No answer. Concern settled over him, but he pushed it away. He hoped she wasn't still in the shower. She'd been late so often. Instead of calling again, he headed for the elevator. If necessary, he would call her from the lobby, but when he stepped into the registration area, Steffi was waiting for him by the door.

He grinned, realizing she had met his need for being on time. Compromise, he thought. Part of a relationship. The thought struck him. Was this a relationship? He felt it growing in his heart. Could it be blossoming in hers?

"Hi," she said. "I'm ready, for a change."

"I noticed."

They went through the doors into the morning sun, and Paul stopped at the curb. "We'll need a taxi for this one."

"It's too far to walk?" Steffi asked.

He nodded and flagged a taxi. Inside the cab, Paul spoke across the seat. "Palazzo Acerbi."

The driver nodded, and Paul settled back, enjoying Steffi's company and watching the landscape pass. He felt relieved that the bustle of the fashion week had reached its end and more so that tomorrow was a new beginning with Steffi.

"I ordered our train tickets for Venice," Paul said. "We pick them up at Central Station tomorrow."

Mentioning the tickets, he noticed her hands tighten in her lap. "Don't worry. Once you're there, things will fall into place. I'm positive."

She sent him a faint grin. "I'm glad you're so confident. I'm still working on courage."

His heart went out to her, but he'd prayed so often that meeting her grandmother would open doors and windows, letting her heart fly free.

"Thanks," she said, shifting her tote bag. "*Palazzo* means palace?"

"Yes, and this one's a beauty. When I realized we were going there, I read about it. It was the home of a marquis in the seventeenth century. Now it's used for exclusive fashion shows like this one."

The cab made a turn and came to a squealing stop. Traffic blocked the thoroughfare and moving ahead looked hopeless. Paul rolled down the window, and exhaust fumes invaded the inside of the taxi. He cranked it closed and breathed a sigh, wondering if they were near the location.

Paul looked at Steffi, and without asking, she gave him a nod, as if she understood. He leaned over the driver's seat. *"Parla inglese?"*

"Sì," the driver said.

"How much further?" Paul asked.

"Two, three blocks," he said, holding up two fingers.

"We'll walk the rest of the way," Paul said, pulling out his wallet and handing the appropriate bills to the driver.

Paul slid out on the curbside and helped Steffi. The driver sat while they moved forward along the rough concrete. Ahead they saw the monumental gate, wide enough for coaches to pass through. When they showed their press cards and entered into the colonnade courtyard, Steffi came to a stop and grabbed his hand with a squeeze.

"It's beautiful." She gestured toward the main rococo staircase decorated with stucco and bronze work.

He agreed, and they followed the crowd upward to the second floor. Paul gaped at the extravagant room. He leaned closer to Steffi. "Do you have your camera?"

She lowered her eyes, then raised them. "I don't need a camera."

"You don't? I thought you always took your own photographs." He remembered the hurt he'd felt when he thought she didn't trust his ability with a camera.

"Not anymore." She gave him a tender smile.

"And why not?"

"Because I have you," she said. She slid her arm around his waist and gave him a squeeze.

Her admission was all he needed to hear. He called that real progress.

Chapter 6

The train swayed as it sped through the Italian countryside, nearly rocking Steffi to sleep. Her mind filled with the wonderful time she'd had in Milan. She'd been pleased with the feature articles she'd sent to the magazine via the Internet, and she'd received accolades that lifted her spirit.

Meeting Paul had been a gift from God. Not only had he been kind and helpful, but also he'd become her friend, one of the best friends she'd had in a long time. She'd always been afraid to form attachments, fearing she would be hurt again. Today Steffi chided herself for her fear. Why hadn't she given the problem to the Lord? Since she'd come to Italy, she'd drawn closer to her faith . . . perhaps an influence of Paul's.

When the train had made a short stop at Verona, Steffi had longed to get off and make her way through the ancient city streets and visit the setting of Shakespeare's play, *Romeo and Juliet*, but time didn't permit. Instead, she'd admired the church steeples and tall fountains visible from the train station.

"How much longer?" she asked Paul. The closer they came to Venice, the more her heart palpitated and her hands trembled.

He grinned. "You sound like a little kid. I don't know, but we're close." He lifted her hand from the armrest and held it in his. "Are you getting nervous?"

"Yes. I suppose it's silly. My grandmother's not waiting for me at the station."

"That's right. We'll get there, and you can take time to collect yourself. I know in my heart, Steffi, that you'll be happy you did this."

"Thanks for your confidence."

She returned her attention to the passing scenery while her mind sorted through a myriad of questions and imaginings, trying to guess what her grandmother would look like and be like. Would she be as loving as her letter indicated? Would she have the answers to the questions that burned in Steffi's heart?

The conductor passed by, calling out, "Venezia." Venice. Steffi's heart stopped, and she caught her breath. She was being foolish, she realized, but anxiety wrapped around her chest like barbed wire.

The train pulsed to a stop, and passengers rose, pulling baggage from overhead bins. Steffi sat still, unable to make her legs move.

Paul rose and stepped into the aisle, then pulled down their carry-ons. "You're staying onboard? Where are you headed? Florence?" His voice was teasing.

She lifted her gaze and tried to smile, but her face had frozen in place. "I'm petrified, Paul."

"We're in Venice," he said, taking her hand and urging her up. "Think of the city, not the mission. You can take a day to catch your breath."

His suggestion made standing easier. Steffi roused herself and slid into the aisle, then grasped her bag and followed him from the train. Outside the air felt damp, and puddles attested to a recent rain. She breathed in the fresh air and watched the sun peek from behind a cloud, sending rays of golden light shimmering into beads of moisture clinging to everything.

She followed Paul as they collected their bags and headed toward the taxi sign. Forgetting where they were, Steffi gawked at the line of people standing along the water's edge. "This is it?"

"Taxi or bus. That's your choice."

"In the water?"

He gave her a poke. "Venice has no streets. I thought you realized that. It has canals. It's water taxis and buses . . . or walk. Those are your choices."

"I never gave that much thought," she said. "I figured we had options . . . like Amsterdam. I'm just surprised."

The line moved closer, and they settled into a water taxi.

"Venezia Splendid Hotel," Paul told the driver.

The man acknowledged him, and Paul moved toward the back. Steffi chuckled when he had to stoop to ease his way beneath the low opening into the interior. They settled on a hard bench inside, and when the taxi filled with eight passengers, they headed along the canal.

The sight was more than Steffi had imagined. Ancient buildings of stone and brick lined the waterway with small piers — some covered with canopies — for passengers to disembark or to wait for a water taxi. Poles lined the dock where boats or gondolas could moor to the building. Shuttered windows, some with small wrought iron balconies, looked out over the winding canal.

They wended their way through narrow

channels with walls so close Steffi could almost touch them. They turned right and left, like city streets flooded with water. Unique bridges, each different in appearance, spanned from one side to the other. Pedestrians passed overhead while some hung over the railing waving to them as they motored beneath. Homes, hotels, apartments, and businesses lined the way, and at an occasional stop, a passenger or two left the taxi.

When the canal widened, Paul squeezed her hand. "This is the Grand Canal."

Steffi eyed the expanse of water, and her pulse raced when the taxi sped past a gondola, with its unique shape like ancient Persian shoes with toes and heels curving upward. The lone oarsman stood at the back, his long pole cutting through the water. He dressed in a black-and-white striped shirt, wearing an Italian sombrero with long black ribbons wrapping the crown and hanging down in back. Steffi had seen them in photographs but never imagined she'd see the real thing.

"This is amazing," she said, her heart in her throat. Yet at the same time, she was filled with sadness. Why couldn't she be this excited to meet her grandmother? She felt her body shrink into the bench, weighted with guilt and sorrow.

"Something wrong?" Paul asked, eyeing her with concern.

She shook her head. "I'm just overwhelmed." Steffi had told the truth, being engulfed in a mix of emotions on both ends of the spectrum.

"You would have missed this if you'd decided not to come. See what God can do." He slid his arm around her shoulders and gave her a squeeze. "He directed you to Venice."

Paul looked sincere, and his words hung in her mind. "Do you really think it was God's work?"

He raised her clasped hand and brought it to his lips. "Steffi, I believe this whole adventure was God's bidding." He lowered his lips and kissed her fingers.

She warmed inside at this gentleness . . . and his faith.

Again they left the Grand Canal and wove their way down another narrow channel. Steffi looked ahead and saw a bright red awning and thin red-and-white poles, like a barbershop.

"Venezia Splendid Hotel," the driver called. The motor rumbled as they stepped from the taxi and loaded their luggage onto the pier. In a moment, the boat sped away, leaving a soft ripple of waves in the brackish water.

Paul gathered his luggage, and she followed, stepping into the hotel — her first step in Venice and her first step toward facing the woman who called herself grandmother. That step was far wider and more frightening than any other Steffi had ever taken.

Paul held the city map he'd been given at the reception desk and gave it a quick look. The streets appeared like a maze, divided only by the snaking width of the Grand Canal.

Steffi eyed the plan and shrugged. "You know me," she said. "I'd get us lost in a minute."

He chuckled as they stepped through the doorway to the outside, his camera hung from his neck on a wide strap. To the left, he spotted a footbridge to allow people across the canal where narrow streets rambled into wider walkways and piazzas. Not one bicycle or motor vehicle interrupted the pedestrian streets. Only the waterways buzzed with the sound of the water vehicles.

He looked to the right, where the sidewalk wended off into a maze, and grasped

Steffi's arm, steering her in that direction. They ambled past glass and silk shops, boutiques, and cafés, stopping on occasion to glance into the colorful windows displaying lace, embroidery, and silk garments. Finally they reached an ornate fountain marking the entrance of Piazza San Marco, the largest square in Venice.

Steffi hurried ahead, like a child chasing the ice cream man, her hair blowing on the breeze and her trim body twirling like a sandstorm. She faced him and ran backward, beckoning him to join her.

Paul hurried to catch up, laughing at her exuberance. When he came to the center of the amazing square, he stopped, letting the magnificence settle over him. Steffi came to his side and slid her hand in his. His heart lifted at her open acceptance. He squeezed her palm, praising God for allowing them this time together in such a perfect place.

After removing his lens cap, Paul framed in the surrounding buildings and artists on the square selling their paintings of well-known Venice scenes. He set up his shot, adjusted the exposure, and captured the moment. When Steffi wasn't looking, he photographed her awed face, taking in the beauty.

Paul replaced his lens cap, and they ambled, hand in hand, to the outside tables that spread along the square. Violinists filled the air with music, and people walked past, taking in the beauty of the day and of the ornate buildings that surrounded the piazza.

"It's breathtaking," Steffi said, gesturing toward the magnificent structures. In front of them stood the Basilica of San Marco — Saint Mark in English. The ornate facade covered with Romanesque carvings had five archways leading into the church. On the right stood the Doges Palace, a gothic structure built of white and pink marble. Paul felt as awed as Steffi, but his masculine pride kept his excitement under control.

"I'd like to go inside the cathedral," Steffi said, asking with her eyes.

He took her hand, and they joined the crowd making their way into the massive edifice. Inside, Paul marveled at the beautiful mosaic columns that lined the walls and the mosaic-tiled floor that echoed the sound of their footsteps. A reverent hush hung over the sanctuary as tourists admired the Byzantine enamel paintings and the goldsmith art that adorned the altar screen. As they crept along, Steffi sank to a pew, her head tilted upward and her face glowing with amazement.

Paul opened his mouth to speak, then closed it, seeing she had bowed her head in prayer. He could only speculate that the prayer related to their quest. He longed to support her and show her how much he cared, but she had to make the decision alone. The delicate balance between finding love and clinging to bitterness was a journey Paul could not walk. Steffi, alone, with the Lord's blessing, had to be moved by the Holy Spirit to gift the older woman with a visit.

Lowering his head, Paul joined in Steffi's prayer. Where two or three are gathered, the Lord had said, and Paul clung to those words of hope.

When Steffi lifted her head, Paul rose, and they wove their way through the transepts and passed in front of exquisite altars, retracing their steps into the pleasant sunshine.

"Well?" Paul asked, having no real question in mind.

"I feel better," she said. "It's not my kind of church, but the magnificence drew me closer to the Lord and helped me imagine how much more glorious heaven will be. It was awesome."

They wandered away from the crowd past the government buildings and headed through the narrow streets to where the Grand Canal twisted through the city. When they reached another stretch of the wide canal, they stopped to watch the gondoliers propel their oars through the water in perfect rhythm.

"I know they're expensive, but I'd love to take a gondola ride," Steffi said, holding her hand above her eyes to block the sun, now low on the horizon.

"One day, maybe you will," he said, knowing he'd planned to do just that.

Paul raised his camera and focused on the gondoliers. When he lowered the lens, a thought struck him. "Let's find a photo shop where I can get these rolls developed. I'm anxious to see them."

Steffi gave him a playful pout. "You hurried me out so fast I didn't bring my camera along."

"Tomorrow's another day, and it'll give us a reason to come back."

She grinned, and he led the way, searching for a professional photo shop. Not too far along the canal, he spotted one. Inside, Paul was pleased to learn they had one-day service. He left the film and walked outside. Drawn by the tempting aroma of pizza drifting from a nearby stand, Paul realized they hadn't eaten for hours. He gestured toward the small café.

"Pizza?" he asked.

"Love it," she said, joining him at the window to order a large slice. They found a table and sat beside the canal. To the east, the Rialto Bridge spanned the wide channel with small shops lining its arch, and to the west, the sinking sun reflected in the calm water.

Steffi took a bite of the cheesy topping, then ran her tongue along her lips to capture the wayward sauce. "Delicious and beautiful, too." Her free hand motioned toward the velvet sunset that spread over the buildings and rippled on the water.

They sat quietly, eating pizza and sipping soft drinks. From across the water, a concertina sent a soft wave of music, and from an occasional gondola, a tenor's voice drifted to their ears, singing an Italian love song. She watched the gondoliers dipping their long oars into the water in an easy rhythm. They stroked and glided with precision — the right depth, the proper speed, confident in knowing the pathways through the maze of canals and sensing the beat and cadence of each stroke.

Sometimes she felt as if she were heading downstream with one oar, unable to keep her boat on course and not always knowing the way. She needed direction and confidence. If only she sat in the passenger seat and let the Lord be her gondolier, she, too, would glide along life's canal knowing she was in good hands. She would have no assurance that her course wouldn't be rough, but with a pilot who knew the way, she would come through it safely. In the hush of conversation, she sent up a prayer, asking God to give her courage to let go and let God be her navigator.

"It's been a perfect day, Paul. I can't imagine what I'd be doing if I was here alone."

"You'd be lost in this maze," he said.

She laughed, and the sound warmed his heart.

"I can't imagine being here without you." He looked into her eyes and, for the first time, saw promise, a hint of hope and happiness he'd never seen before.

Paul slipped her hand in his and felt the quiet ticking of her pulse. They gazed at each other as the sun touched the rooftops, then sank below them, leaving only a shimmer of gold on the red tiles.

When the cooler air drifted off the water,

Paul stood and Steffi joined him. No longer shy, he held her hand as they wove their way back to the hotel.

"What did you plan for tomorrow?" Paul asked, hoping the Lord had guided her answer.

"I–I'm not sure," she murmured. "I'm thinking about it."

"And praying?"

She gave him a crooked grin. "And praying about it."

"It's the only way, *cara mia.*"

The tender words sprang from his heart, and Steffi's loving look lighted the evening darkness.

Chapter 7

Steffi stood in the window of her hotel room, looking at the canal that passed beneath her window. The moon lay like soft satin on the water, beautiful but leaving her with a sense of melancholy. Now she wished she had opened her heart to Paul and told him the fears that punctured her resolve. In her heart, she had come to meet her grandmother, and now she felt herself backing away from her purpose.

Closing the curtain, Steffi forced herself away from the window and sank onto the bed. She wanted to talk. Would Paul be asleep? She peered at her watch and gave a ragged sigh. *Have faith,* an inner voice whispered. The words startled her.

She walked to the telephone and punched in Paul's room number.

He answered in a heartbeat.

"It's me," she said.

"Hi. Can't sleep?"

"I'm doing the thinking I mentioned."

"How about the praying?" he asked.

His question knocked the air out of her.

She'd already forgotten her promise to pray. "Guess I let that one slip."

"Time you changed."

His voice sounded gentle without reprimand, and she sensed he understood. "Pray for me, Paul. I need to let God take charge."

"You got it, my sweet."

"And speaking of help." She hesitated, knowing what she was going to ask, and drew in a calming breath. "Are you still dressed? Do you have time to talk?"

"Always. How about the café downstairs?"

"Thanks. I'll be there in a minute." She hung up the phone and grabbed her handbag.

Paul was waiting when she arrived. "I shouldn't have dragged you down here."

His tender look surprised her. "Losing your courage?"

He knew her too well. "Let's walk. Anywhere."

Paul nodded, and she suspected he knew she wanted the cover of darkness to ease the conversation.

They left the hotel and followed the walkway to San Marco Piazza. As they walked, Paul held her hand, and his touch brought her comfort. Entering the piazza, they found a bench near the fountain away from the bustle of the square. In the shadows, Steffi felt protected.

Paul slid his arm around her shoulders and drew her closer. "You need to talk, *cara mia*."

The loving phrase wrapped around her heart, and the fears that had weighted her spirit lifted, allowing her tongue to release it. "You're getting to know me too well."

"Never," he said, nuzzling her closer to his shoulder.

She found courage to gaze into his eyes. Though dimmed by the darkness, his concern — his gentle look — gave her confidence. "I've lived in fear of rejection, Paul. I've pushed people away all my life before they abandoned me. I realize why, and I know it's not logical, but I was ingrained to feel bitterness and to dwell on rejection. My mother didn't mean to do that, I know, but it happened."

He didn't speak, but his silent touch let her know he was listening and feeling her emotion.

"When I get close to people, I hold my breath waiting for them to find out that horrible flaw I must have to chase them away." Her voice quivered, and she knew she was losing control.

Paul grasped her hands in his. "You know better. I learned to enjoy your flaws."

The lighthearted tone gave her a moment's reprieve from her sorrow. "Thanks, and I like yours."

His smile faded and a serious expression took its place. "Remember. You've been open enough to tell me this, and I thank the Lord that you have. It's what I've been praying for. You're changing, and you're growing."

He had been honest, and she wanted to give him a straight answer. "That's because I trust you. You're different and special."

"And so are you. God has made us all such wonderful promises. All we need to do is believe in them. In Romans, He tells us that all trials and tribulations are conquerable through Christ's love. You just need to have faith."

"My good sense does, but my irrational mind says no."

"Do you know what you've done all these years?"

Steffi shook her head.

"You've closed the door of your heart and bolted it, fearing who might come in. You've locked out not only the enemy but also friends. Jesus has knocked on your door, but fear has kept you from letting

Him in. You've closed the door to love, Steffi."

He drew her around to face him, his eyes filled with sadness. "How can anyone let you know how much you mean to them when you hide behind a locked door? Open it, *cara mia*."

Tears welled in her eyes and rolled down her cheeks. Paul had been right. He'd seen through her scam of confidence; he'd understood her attempts to protect herself in shapeless clothes; he'd recognized her deep yearning to be loved. She'd spent her life feeling unhappy and insecure. Today was a first step. Paul had given her the key, and God would help her open the door.

"Everything you've said is true." She touched his face, feeling the prickle of a growing beard. "How can I thank you?"

He looked at her without response, and her heart froze for a moment, wondering. Then he captured her hand in his and kissed her fingers. "This is all the thanks I want . . . just looking into your eyes."

She sensed it coming. His lips neared hers, and she greeted them with pleasure, her spirit soaring at his touch. His mouth moved in a gentle caress, and she returned the kiss, enjoying the sense of joy and friendship that they shared.

Tomorrow. A new beginning. A new day. She'd made her decision.

Paul stood beside Steffi in her hotel room, his hand resting on her back to give her courage. He watched her fingers tremble as she punched in the numbers on the telephone. When she told him in the morning she would call her grandmother, he could not describe the joy. In his heart, he knew it was not only the right thing to do but that it was the key to opening the door for Steffi.

"Are you sure you don't want me to leave?" he asked, feeling uneasy about listening to her first conversation with her grandmother.

She shook her head, her ear pressed to the receiver.

Though he preferred to give her privacy, he stayed, as she wanted. He watched Steffi with her ear pressed to the receiver, and from the look on her face, Paul knew when someone had answered the telephone.

"Donata Rosetti, *grazie*." Steffi hesitated. "Oh . . . *buona sera*." She gave Paul a frantic look. "This is Steffi Rosetti . . . your granddaughter."

Her face paled while her eyes misted

with tears. She stared at the receiver, then covered the mouthpiece, tears rolling down her face. "What should I do? She's crying."

Paul closed the distance between them and held her close. Her body trembled as she clung to him. "Talk to her, Steffi." He caressed her cheek and wiped away the moisture.

She pulled her hand away and spoke. "I'm in Venice with a friend. I've come to see you."

Her voice quavered, and watching the scene tore at Paul's heart. Though he couldn't hear the grandmother's words, he could sense her joy. Steffi's tension seemed to ebb as she spoke, and Paul shifted away again, praising God that she had chosen to take the path toward healing.

He sat on the only chair in the room, and when he refocused on Steffi, she was beckoning to him.

"Would you talk to her and get directions?" Though tears misted her eyes, she gave him a faint smile. "You know me."

He did know her and realized Steffi would never find the way to her grandmother's house alone. Paul took the receiver and spoke to Donata Rosetti. Though the woman had a strong Italian accent, she spoke in almost perfect English, and while he waited, Steffi scrambled for a scrap of paper, and he scribbled the directions to her villa in the Santa Croce district.

When he'd finished, Paul returned the telephone to Steffi, and she set a time then said good-bye. She placed the receiver in the cradle and turned to face him.

He saw it coming. The flood of joy and sorrow she'd controlled broke from its well and spilled down her cheeks. She rushed to Paul's arms, and he nestled her close as she sobbed on his shoulder. When Steffi calmed, she lifted her head and used his handkerchief to wipe her eyes.

"I'm sorry. It's —"

"Don't feel embarrassed. It's natural to cry," he said. "Your grandmother sounded thrilled. You've brought her joy . . . just by your telephone call."

"I know, but —"

He pressed a finger to her lips to halt her apology. He meant what he'd said. "What time is she expecting you?"

"For lunch . . . at one."

"I'll walk you there. Hopefully you can find your way back." He asked God's assistance on that one. The thought caused a grin.

"Why are you smiling?" she asked.

He caressed her cheek. "I'm happy for you, *cara mia*."

Steffi lingered on the sidewalk outside her grandmother's home. She'd never been to a villa and had no idea what to expect. She gazed outside the gray stone building, adorned with only slate-colored window shutters and door. Steffi read the address on the building again to make certain she hadn't made a mistake. Anxiety tugged at her nerves and tightened her chest. Her grandmother had sounded warm and loving on the telephone, and Steffi's heart had opened to the woman, but she'd learned that life held surprises — some bad and some good, and Steffi wasn't confident that the welcome wouldn't change to feelings she didn't want to face.

"Go ahead," Paul said, standing near the bell. "Ring it. You'll never meet her this way."

"Maybe that's for the best." She rubbed her hand along the tight cords of her neck. "I really want to leave."

"No, you don't." He stepped closer and, in the empty street, brushed a kiss across her lips. "You're here now. Have faith." His gentle touch sent a comforting warmth coursing through her chest, unleashing some of her fear.

She studied Paul's sincere face and gentle gaze. Harnessing courage, she stepped forward and pushed the bell.

"I'm proud of you." He squeezed her arm. "I'm leaving now, and I'll see you back at the hotel."

"No, don't go. I'll never make it back without you."

"Yes, you will. Straight down this sidewalk to the canal and a left will lead you to a water taxi or bus. They'll drop you off at the hotel dock."

"But —"

Her sentence was shortened by a noise at the door. Before she could move, an elderly woman swung open the gate and stood in the threshold, her eyes wide and pooled with tears. Steffi had no doubt. She recognized her father's features in the woman's face — her father's face she'd seen only in a single photograph now brought to life in the lean, attractive woman.

No words passed between them. Donata Rosetti opened her arms, and Steffi stepped into the embrace. The movement seemed so natural and felt so right.

"It has been too long. Too long," her

grandmother said, her eyes searching Steffi's face, her voice trembling with emotion. "I've waited a lifetime for this moment."

Steffi nodded, unable to speak without sobs bursting from her bound chest. When she found her voice, she gestured toward Paul. "This is my friend, Paul DiAngelo." The words caught in her throat. "This is my grandmother," she said to Paul.

Donata greeted him, then took Steffi's hand and led her forward. "Come in . . . both of you."

Paul shifted back, then remembered his manners. "Thank you, Signora Rosetti. I wanted to make sure Steffi arrived here safely. I'm heading back to the hotel."

Steffi looked at him with longing, wanting him to stay, but she had no right to invite him in.

"No," Donata said, beckoning to him. "I have too much food for two ladies. Please, join us for lunch. It is nearly ready."

She stretched out her arm to him, and Steffi relaxed when she saw Paul step toward her and follow them through the doorway.

Inside the courtyard, Steffi faltered. From the outside, she hadn't expected such charm. In the center of the yard, beds of flowers surrounded an ornate fountain. Two shade trees stood near the U-shaped house, their branches giving shade to a wrought-iron table, bench, and chairs. A cobblestone path circled the yard and led to an arched doorway.

"This is lovely," Steffi said.

"This was your father's home." Her grandmother's voice was weighted with sadness.

Hearing reference to her father, Steffi's heart knotted, and a thin edge of fear worked its way into her thoughts.

"Come," Donata said, opening the thick wooden door.

As soon as Steffi stepped inside, luscious scents of meat and sauce drifted from the kitchen. The foyer opened to a large living room with furnishings that had probably been in the home for many years — sturdy and well crafted. Donata motioned them inside, and they seated themselves on a tapestry sofa while she excused herself for the kitchen.

Steffi drew in a deep breath and looked at Paul. "I can't believe I'm here. Thank you for prodding me to come."

"God did all the work. I had little to do with it."

Steffi knew it was God's work, but Paul's

faith and confidence had helped her more than she could say.

Within a few minutes, Donata returned and beckoned them into her dining room. An antique buffet and sturdy table shone with china and crystal. They gathered around the table, and Donata prayed, praising God for Steffi's visit. Anticipating their upcoming conversation, Steffi had a difficult time swallowing the wonderful food her grandmother had prepared. Yet Steffi grinned watching Paul enjoy the feast that arrived at the table in such abundance — salads, pasta, anti-pasto, chicken, roasted potatoes, fruit, and cheese. When the last course had ended, Donata rose and invited them into the living room.

"If you don't mind," Paul said, "I'd like to walk for awhile." He gave them a wry grin as if admitting his reason. "You both have years to cover, and I'd like to give you some time alone."

"Paul, you don't have to —" Steffi touched his arm.

"I don't have to. I want to," he said. "I'll enjoy the fresh air."

Steffi knew she was defeated, and with a wave, Paul stepped outside. Through the open window, she heard the street door swing closed.

"Why not enjoy the sunshine, too?" Donata said, rising. "Let's go into the garden."

Steffi rose and followed her grandmother into the courtyard. She led her to the chairs beneath the tree. Steffi selected a chair in the sunlight, while her grandmother settled onto a wrought-iron bench in the shade.

Donata turned her face toward the outside door and gestured. "He seems like a fine young man." Her tender gaze filled with understanding.

"He's wonderful. We don't know each other well, but we will." Feeling she needed to explain, Steffi told her grandmother about her work at *Mode* and how she'd met Paul.

"Surely the Lord's doing," Donata said, her slender hands clasped in her lap as if in prayer.

Steffi's pulse skipped, hearing her grandmother's reference to her faith. She knew so little. "Was my father a believer?"

Her grandmother's face grew melancholy. "Your father was a wonderful man who knew the Lord well. He was a good man, Steffi, and he loved you dearly."

The unexpected words rattled through her and shook her to the core. Steffi knew she should take her time and allow her grandmother to speak at leisure, but couldn't hold back her curiosity. "I don't understand how he could love me and . . ." She let the words trail off, seeing the look that filled her grandmother's eyes.

"So much sorrow has passed through this house," Donata said. "Your father not only loved you, he loved your mother."

As if struck by a hammer, Steffi winced with confusion and disbelief. How could this be? She searched her grandmother's face, looking for an explanation. "But how can that be? Why was he here and not in New York City?"

"Sit here beside me," Donata said, patting the bench seat. "Let me tell you about your father and the love he had."

Her grandmother's look drew Steffi from the safety of the chair. She rose, her heels clicking on the cobblestone, and settled beside her grandmother. The older woman clasped Steffi's hand in hers. Donata's skin was creped with age but as soft as velvet.

"Your grandfather, Rocco, was a good man. Hardworking. Generous. He loved children, but the Lord only blessed us with one, your father, Antonio. We called him Tony. He gave us such joy, and when he was ready for college, your grandfather allowed him to go to America for his education. That's where he met your mother."

Steffi listened, her mind filled with questions.

"My Rocco had a good business head. He bought land outside of Venice and grew olive trees. Rosetti Olive Oil was the best, and the business grew to be successful. He bought this villa, and he could afford a college education for Antonio in the United States.

"We were disappointed when Tony called to say he had fallen in love with a beautiful American woman." She lifted her hand and guided Steffi's face toward her. "You must have your mother's eyes, but you are so like your father. He was a handsome man."

"I don't remember him," Steffi said, "but my mother always said he was good-looking."

"When you were a baby, your grandfather died, and since your father was our only son, I asked him to bring his family here so he could take over the business." Donata tapped two fingers against her temple. "I have no business sense, and I didn't know what to do."

The news inched into Steffi's mind. She had never known the reason her father had abandoned her. "But why didn't he bring us here? Why didn't we hear from him?"

Her grandmother patted Steffi's hand. "Your father told your mother about his homeland. You see how beautiful it is in Italy . . . and Venice is most lovely."

"It's charming," Steffi said. "It's a city of romance."

"Ahh, yes. The city of romance. Tony tried to convince your mother to come to Italy. She told him to go and promised she would follow."

Promised she would follow. "Are you sure?" Steffi asked.

"As sure as my heart beats. I overheard his telephone calls. I saw the tears in his eyes through the tears in my own. I had never met your mother . . . only through photographs."

Sorrow knotted in Steffi's chest. "I only saw one photograph of my father."

"Only one? I have many, Steffi. I will show you." She rose. Her face looked tired. Steffi knew the stress of their meeting had taken its toll on both of them.

Donata went into the house and returned with a thick album. Steffi held the book in her lap, and as she turned the pages, her heart leaped with each photograph — snapshots of her father as a child and another as a teen working amidst the olive trees. She drew the album nearer, seeing one of her father and mother looking into each others eyes, their love so evident. The vision touched her but left her bewildered.

"Your father sent us these pictures from America. New York," Donata said, running her finger over the photo in a caress.

Steffi pressed her hand against her heart and turned the page. She faltered while tears rose in her eyes and blurred the photograph — her mother stood beside her father holding Steffi, a toddler, in his arms, his face beaming at her. She tried to speak but only tears flowed.

Donata drew her closer, and they let the years of hurt and sadness flow from their heart in the form of tears.

When Steffi gained control, she wiped her eyes and studied the snapshot. The look of tenderness dumbfounded her. Her father loved her. She saw it in his face.

"This picture was taken shortly before your father came back to Italy," Donata said. "He brought the photos with him."

Steffi studied the images, admiring his strong build and his classic features, but most of all, she cherished the look in his eyes as he gazed at her in the photograph.

"This was the last picture I saw of you," Donata said.

Overwhelmed, Steffi sat a moment trying to gather her thoughts and settle the questions that had lain on her heart all her life. Despite the unknown details that still remained, she knew that her father loved her. "If he loved me, I don't understand why he didn't keep in touch and why I never heard from him when I grew old enough."

"You were never abandoned by your father, dearest Steffi . . . not your earthly father or your Father in heaven who has watched over you these many years. When your father could not be with you, he kept you in his prayers and in God's loving hands."

Confusion rattled through Steffi, wanting to comprehend and wanting to believe.

Donata lifted her finger and rose. "Come with me. Bring the album with you." Steffi nestled the photographs in her arms and followed her grandmother into the house. While Donata made her way across the room, Steffi returned to the love seat, still clutching the album. She ran her hand across the smooth leather, then placed it on the table in front of her.

She watched her grandmother bend to

open a door beneath a large cabinet against the wall. When she returned, Steffi saw she carried a box. Donata placed it in Steffi's lap, then sank beside her. "Open the box. It will answer your questions."

Her hands shaking, Steffi lifted the lid and looked inside. A bundle of letters filled the bottom, and her heart lurched when she focused on the handwriting. Her mother's address was written on the front with bold strokes. The return address was this one — the villa. Steffi stared at the letters, postmarked and stamped, but marked return to sender.

"He wrote to us, and my mother sent them back?" Unable to handle the new information, Steffi closed her eyes, trying to comprehend what it all meant.

"I took the liberty to open these after your father died," Donata said. "Your father was adamant that I not interfere in your mother's life . . . or yours. He was a beaten man." Donata drew closer to Steffi and rested a hand on her shoulder. "My front door and my heart have always been open to you." She clasped her free hand to her chest. "I so wanted to offer the invitation, but I honored your father's wishes, but now, it is different. You are here."

With tears pooling in her eyes, Steffi

grasped her grandmother's hand and pressed it to her cheek, then shifted her gaze to the box. Steffi lifted one of the yellowed envelopes and studied the date. She selected another. Time after time her father had written, and the letters were returned unopened.

"He never divorced your mother," Donata said. "Your father remained faithful to her all of his life."

The tears that rimmed Steffi's eyes rolled down her cheeks and dripped on the yellowed paper. "May I read one?"

"Read them all, my dear. They will help you to know that your father loved you both. The answers — if there are any — rest with your mother, but let me say one thing." Her grandmother touched Steffi's hand again, then clasped it between hers. "I forgive your mother. I trust she had her reasons, whatever they may be. God tells us to forgive so that our sins may be forgiven. We have all sinned. We have all made mistakes. I may never understand what happened in the United States, but I no longer need to know. I'm so filled with joy to meet you at last."

Steffi held her grandmother's hand and leaned over to kiss her cheek. Like a healing balm, the moment spread over her and cleansed her heart.

When Paul returned, Steffi was still reading the letters. In them, she heard the love and devotion her father held for them. She had felt his plight and experienced how his yearning turned to despair, then to sorrow until finally he'd lost hope. The last letter had been dated the year Steffi had turned fourteen.

"I'll make tea," Donata said, leaving them alone.

"Are you okay?" Paul asked, his face filled with concern.

Her eyes blurred again, and she nodded until she contained her emotions. "I'm fine." But the word seemed so inadequate. "Not fine. I'm much more than fine. I'm whole."

Paul's worried face brightened as he moved to her side and kissed her cheek. "I've prayed for this. All the time I walked, I asked God to help you find the answers."

"I found more than answers. I found healing . . . and forgiveness."

Chapter 8

Steffi walked beside Paul, her hand in his. The afternoon with her grandmother had been more than she had dreamed, and she'd left with promises to return to spend the following day. She and her grandmother had so many years to share in such a short visit.

As they ambled along the sun-warmed streets, Steffi told Paul all that she'd learned. In her shoulder bag, she carried photographs of her father that her grandmother had insisted she take with her — photographs to help her get to know the father she never knew.

"I wish I'd known him," Steffi said, weighted by melancholy.

"You do," Paul said, squeezing her hand. "Through your grandmother's eyes and in your own. She opened the door to the past and let you in. When I look at the photos, I can see your father in you."

She was touched by his thoughts. "Time seems so short, though. Three days to share a lifetime is impossible."

"Now that you've met, you can come

anytime. Your grandmother would love it . . . and maybe one day she could come to New York to visit you."

Steffi couldn't imagine her grandmother in the bustle of New York City, but perhaps it was possible. Her grandmother had spunk and perseverance. She could do just about anything if she set her mind to it. Her letter to Steffi attested to that. "Today has been . . ." She paused unable to express the joy she'd felt.

Paul slid his arm around her shoulder and didn't try to find the words. Steffi knew he understood, and no words could express her gratefulness to God and the healing that she'd felt after so many years of sorrow and bitterness.

"Thanks for being here and letting me share all this," she said, gazing at his face, haloed by the setting sun.

"Coming here was an honor, and I mean that." Paul watched Steffi's gaze shift behind him, and he turned to catch the golden colors melting on red-tile rooftops and reflecting in the gray water of the canal. He raised her hand to his mouth and kissed her fingers. "I have an idea . . . the perfect way to top off an exceptional afternoon."

Steffi gave him a questioning look, but

he didn't respond. Instead he drew her forward, weaving their way through the narrow walkways with shops on each side selling Murano glass and Italian silk. The walks opened to a small piazza beside the Grand Canal. Paul moved her forward.

"Get in line," he said.

"In line?" She swung her arm forward. "For the gondolas?"

He saw the excitement in her face. "Yes. It's my treat."

"It's too expensive. You've done too much for me already."

"You let me be the judge of that." Paul grinned and urged her forward.

When they reached the front of the line, the boatman helped Steffi into the gondola.

"Venice Hotel Splendid," Paul said.

Walking carefully, Steffi made her way across the flat bottom to the upholstered chair covered with teal fabric and fringe. Paul followed, helping her sit. When he settled into the seat beside her, he pointed to the bow of the barge, where a crystal vase had been attached and held a bouquet of yellow flowers.

"Pretty," Steffi said.

"And romantic," Paul added.

The gondolier pushed away from the

pier. With his single oar, he steered the barge into the center of the Grand Canal. Paul slipped his arm around Steffi's shoulders, and she nestled closer as they glided along the canal with only distant music and the dip of an oar breaking the silence.

The colors of the sunset spread along the water like an artist's palette, daubed by the shimmer of red, white, and brown brick buildings standing on the water's edge, and in the distance, the white arches of the Rialto Bridge neared.

In time, the gondola followed the twisting path and glided past San Marco Piazza, and in the sinking sun, lights of buildings came on along the canal, adding a sprinkle of glitter to the darkening water.

"Paul, this is beautiful. It is a perfect ending to a perfect day."

"Not an ending. Remember? It's only the beginning."

Awareness shuffled across her face, and she nodded. "A special beginning."

The gondola veered left and floated from the Grand Canal to a narrow waterway, heading toward their hotel.

"What's that?" Steffi asked, pointing to an ornate enclosed bridge that spanned the canal and connected two gray brick buildings. Two wrought iron-covered windows looked out over the canal. "I've never seen a bridge like that one."

"It's the Bridge of Sighs. Many years ago, the bridge was used to transport prisoners to the place of execution."

Her smile faded. "I suppose it was the prisoners' sighs that gave it the name. That's sad."

"Now it's just a beautiful bridge not used for prisoners anymore," he said, hoping to cheer her. He felt her shoulders relax.

"You know, today was like getting out of prison for me," Steffi said. "Finally, I'm free. I've unlocked the door that I kept closed so long."

"You've unlocked another door, too."

She tilted her head and gazed at him. "My grandmother's?"

He grinned. "Her, too, but I meant me, Steffi. You've unlocked the door to my heart. I've prayed for days that you'd feel the same."

"I do, Paul. You're wonderful. You've helped me find my way around Milan and Venice . . . and now, you've helped me find my way home to my grandmother. I don't think I'd have done it without you."

"I think you would have. God wanted it to be. You came all this way. I don't think you'd have given up."

"Maybe you're right, but you've become so important to me. Sometimes I wonder if God had this all set up."

Paul chuckled. "I've said that to myself so many times. The Lord works miracles and opens windows and doors. I realize we've only known each other a couple of weeks, but look how it worked out."

"We both work at *Mode* and spend our time in Manhattan," she said.

"God's fixed it so we have time to get to know each other better, but . . . to be honest, I know I've fallen in love with you."

"And I love you, Paul. You're the key to my heart."

A tenor's voice drifted across the water, his love song intermingled with the music of a concertina, while Paul drew Steffi into his arms and kissed her. His heart surged with the feeling of her lips on his and the beating of her heart against his chest. God had guided them to find each other and opened the doors of their hearts.

Dear Reader,

Two years ago, my husband, Bob, and I left our home in Lathrup Village, Michigan, and stepped off an airplane in Milan, Italy. There, we began our journey, visiting so many well-known cities such as: Venice, Florence, Rome, Pisa, Naples, Sorrento, Pompeii, and the Isle of Capri. As we entered some of the glorious churches, we were awed by the magnificent Christian art work created by such men as Michelangelo and DaVinci. We were amazed at the power we saw in the statue of David and the beauty of the ceiling in the Sistine Chapel. We stood beside DaVinci's *The Last Supper* and viewed the bell tower the world knows as the Leaning Tower of Pisa.

I am always awed by God's good gifts to us, including our talents. When I began writing fiction in 1997, I had no idea what abundant blessings the Lord would give me. I was published with Heartsong Presents in 1998 and since have signed contracts for thirty-one novels or novellas. The Lord has allowed me to witness about Him through stories that make people laugh and cry, stories that touch hearts and lives with the glorious truth of our salvation through Christ Jesus. I praise God daily for His abundant blessings.

Visit my web site and view the photographs of our trip to Italy under the section called About Me. I love to hear from you. So please drop me a line and say hello. I wish you God's richest blessings.

In Him,
Gail Gaymer Martin

The Lure
of Capri

DiAnn Mills

Dedication

To Beau and Allison for all of their
research and help.

Prologue

Terri Donatelli blew the dust from her great-grandmother's worn leather Bible and reached inside for the familiar yellowed slip of paper. She'd read the Italian words hundreds of times until she had them memorized. Each twist of the pen had drawn Terri into the world of her great-grandmother in the early 1900s on the Isle of Capri and the anguish of lost love.

Taking a deep breath, Terri unfolded the fragile letter.

My darling Giovanni,

How foolish and wrong I've been. Please forgive me for the pain I've caused you. Believe me, I never meant to hurt you. You brought so much love and laughter into my life, a precious gift from heaven, and all I've offered in return is heartache. You gave me your heart and a promise of a lifetime of devotion. I gave you tears and pleadings for you to join me in Venice. Always I begged for my way until now I fear it is too late. My selfishness eats at my soul; my tears declare my guilt. My joy, my love, I pray you still have love for me.

I thought I couldn't leave my family, but God in His infinite wisdom has shown me I can do anything with Him. Giovanni, we can be together, forever as God intended. I love you more than life, and I want to live out my days with you. I pray this is not too late.

Visions of Capri are before me. I remember the sound of the waves breaking against the shore, the salty scent of the blue Mediterranean, the cry of the seagulls, and the lure of the mountain peaks. Most of all, I remember your arms around me asking me to be your wife.

Oh, how you have captivated me along with the beauty of the island. Please answer me, my Giovanni! I long to be with you. Tell me you still love me!

Teresa

Chapter 1

Terri Donatelli stared at the colorful travel brochure describing the Isle of Capri and realized she might never return to Kentucky. She'd dreamed of this trip since high school, and tomorrow she'd actually board a plane en route to this ancient island. There, she'd live for a month among her ancestry. A fluttering exploded in her stomach at the mere thought.

Terri lived with the knowledge — and sometimes the loud and crazy antics — of a large Italian family. She loved them fiercely, and she understood their protective nature. But only when her great-grandmother revealed the beauty of the Isle of Capri and the story of her first love, did Terri appreciate her heritage. The island drew her to explore all of its charm, wonder, and the exquisite people.

Her great-grandmother's recollections came alive with sights, sounds, and the anticipation of smells and tastes that surpassed any book or picture. Unfortunately, Teresa Donatelli passed away the summer after Terri's freshman year in high school, but the faded and worn letter to her first love lived on in the old, Italian Bible passed on to Terri.

Placing the travel brochure on her bed alongside her passport, airline tickets, and travel itinerary, Terri glanced at her cell phone and knew she had to call Ryan. The dreaded call had loomed over her the past week. Ryan had discovered her plans for a summer vacation to Capri, but he didn't know her departure date. Once she told him, he'd be considerate and shy away from any confrontation, but deep inside he'd be devastated. If she took the initiative to probe deeper, he'd admit his worrisome nature and his reluctance to let her go. Separating herself from Ryan Stevens was the only part of the trip that her family supported.

"Maybe you can find an Italian husband," her father said the previous night. "You certainly can't find one here in Louisville." Naturally, he made the comment while her older brother visited with his four boisterous sons.

Maybe God did plan for her to fall in love with a handsome Italian. What a legacy her great-grandmother had left for her. Giovanni might live on after all!

"Dad, I want to see Capri as Grandmother Teresa did. I don't know if anything else will happen. I'm going for the experience, not to find a husband."

"Sounds like a bad idea to me," Dominic said, a replica of their father, with high cheekbones and large dark eyes. "Who is looking after you?"

"I'm with a Christian tour group, and in case you haven't noticed, I'm a college professor with plenty of intellect to take care of myself."

"You should be raising kids." Dad lifted baby Josh onto his lap.

"Hush," her mother said, scooping up the toys from the floor. "Terri has prayed about this, and she believes God wants her to take the trip."

"At least Ryan is not in the picture," Dad said. "Nice man, but not Italian."

Later, Dad found her alone in the kitchen and gathered her into his arms. He smelled of spice and garlic, and she loved it. "My sweet Terri, I want you to be happy. Naturally, I think you would be happier with an Italian man, but I want the man God wants for you. Am I forgiven for what I said about Ryan?"

"Of course. I love you, too, Daddy. I'll have a wonderful time and take lots of pictures."

"You are too much like my grandmother — ready to take on the world." He planted a kiss on the tip of her nose. "How does Ryan feel about your leaving?"

Terri hesitated. "I haven't told him yet."

Dad's huge shoulders raised and lowered. "Terri, he has a right to know. I've seen the way he looks at you. Honey, I'm disappointed. That man is going to be hurt."

"I'll tell him tomorrow night. I promise."

This was tomorrow night. Terri snatched up the phone and stared at the numbers. A big part of her wished Ryan wouldn't answer, but prolonging the inevitable made matters worse. He deserved to hear her plans. She owed him that.

Ryan Stevens taught English at the same university where she taught Italian. She'd met him three years ago, and instantly his considerate, thoughtful mannerisms attracted her. At the time, two popular coeds had cornered a young man who lacked social skills. They were teasing him about dating a sorority sister, and all he could do was stammer. Just when Terri stood ready to give the girls a lesson in propriety, Ryan stepped forward.

"Ladies, I'm sure this guy is flattered with your attention, but since he outdid both of you last semester, give him a break. He has better things to do." Ryan proceeded to escort the coeds to the end of the hall.

Later, when the young man disappeared, she congratulated Ryan on his rescue mission.

"Those two have no idea the damage they're doing to a shy kid who is speechless around a pretty face. Besides, they were brought up in church and understand perfectly what our Lord expects from us." He chuckled, and his green eyes sparkled. "I have them in my college Sunday school class and know their parents." He stuck out his hand. "I'm Ryan Stevens."

Terri smiled and introduced herself. "I started teaching Italian this semester."

"I know. I've been looking for a way to meet you."

Flattered, Terri braved forward. "How about coffee?"

Terri and Ryan had been together ever since. Their friends called them comfortable opposites, extreme personalities that appeared to balance. She lived up to every story about volatile Italians, while he never allowed things to bother him.

Ryan hadn't mentioned love, no doubt waiting for her to make the first move. His reluctance to initiate anything frustrated her, but he could be sweet with unexpected flowers and special gifts. Sometimes Terri's demonstrative family threatened her sanity, but Ryan always calmed her with infinite patience. On the flip side, Ryan's unpredictable moodiness drove her to distraction. Clamming up and preferring solitude when she loved the mere sight of people sometimes caused arguments. Left to him, she felt sure they'd date forever, when in fact she wanted to be wooed and wowed to the altar.

Terri wanted more from a relationship than an introvert and an extrovert seeking stable ground. Terri craved excitement and adventure, and she'd find it for sure in Capri. Without another moment's delay, she speed dialed Ryan's phone.

"Hey, what's happening in your world?" she asked.

"I might ask the same," he said.

She heard the edge in his voice. "Sounds like you're in a great mood."

"I'm trying to be."

"Ryan, what's wrong? You know how I hate to play games."

He expelled a heavy sigh. "I'm not the game player here. I saw your sister today, and she asked me how I felt about your upcoming vacation."

Terri inwardly groaned. "My trip is why I'm calling."

"To say good-bye before you whisk away to Italy?"

"You're not being fair. You knew I was going to Capri this summer." She should be apologizing, but the words refused to form.

"I see a big difference between talking about a trip and making the travel arrangements without informing me. I thought we had better communication than this."

Guilt assaulted her, but not enough to take total blame. "Maybe if you had encouraged me to pursue my dreams, I wouldn't have kept it from you."

"And I thought we'd honeymoon in Capri — visit the spots your great-grandmother spoke about."

His words stunned her and irritated her at the same time. "How nice to inform me. And when did you plan the wedding? Was this before or after your declaration of love?" Instantly she regretted her outburst. "I'm sorry, Ryan." She plopped down on the bed. "I'm behaving like a spoiled kid. Please forgive me. I intended to tell you weeks ago about the trip, but I assumed you'd try to stop me."

She heard his radio playing contemporary Christian music in the background. The song spoke about finding time in a busy schedule for God.

"I'm sorry, too. Honestly, I'm disappointed, and I don't understand your obsession with the island."

"You never have."

She heard the music lower. "Do you think you'll find the man of your dreams there, like your great-grandmother left behind?" She envisioned his eyes narrowing and his fingers combing through amber-colored hair.

"Ryan." She stopped the flow of words before she did more damage. Actually, his question hit closer to the truth than she wanted to admit.

"For what it's worth, I love you."

Why didn't he tell her sooner? "I don't know what to say." Why couldn't he have planned a romantic dinner with music and candlelight, instead of blurting it out in the near heat of an argument? She couldn't appreciate the words without atmosphere.

"What time is your flight? I'd like to take you to the airport," Ryan said.

As usual, we don't talk about the real issue. "I need to be there around ten in the morning."

Right then Terri believed she'd made the right decision in not telling Ryan sooner. She didn't want to be around when he withdrew into his little moody world.

Now Ryan understood Terri's moodiness over the past few weeks. He thought she'd planned to break off their relationship. In reality she had. He tried to give her space, honor her independence, and not smother her, but most of the time she interpreted his responses as indifferent. On the other hand, when he began deep subjects about their relationship, she took two steps backward by claiming he didn't understand her.

He hoped this separation sealed their relationship and didn't destroy it. He'd prayed about his love for her and planned a proposal complete with a honeymoon package to Capri. Better Terri be sure about them than hold on to this fairy tale of everlasting love in the arms of an olive-skinned Italian.

On Saturday morning, as he drove to Terri's house with her favorite coffee drink safely in tow, he talked himself into optimism. He did love this woman, even if the right words never formed his heartfelt emotion. For certain, a month without her would be endless, but he could utilize the time to plan for a dynamic proposal — one he knew she dreamed of.

Terri possessed a vivacious love for life that he wished fell in his gene pool. He treasured the intensity of her olive-colored skin, smoldering, dark eyes veiled in a curtain of lashes, and lips perpetually curved in a smile. They quarreled occasionally, but their differences were what he valued about their relationship. Granted she loved people and thrived on them, while he preferred quiet times with dinner or a play, but he could fit into either situation. Terri called him the balanced one. Ryan smiled. Definitely he'd miss her, and he could only pray God brought them back together in a solid relationship.

Once he pulled into her driveway, he laughed aloud at the cars parked up and down the street. Every relative in Louisville must have shown up to wish her bon voyage. He shouldn't be so amused. His family lived in the hills of Kentucky, and he found new cousins at each family reunion. Both sets of families were ready to get together at a moment's notice.

"Hi, Ryan." Dominic Donatelli, Terri's dad, answered the door. "We're having a little going away party for Terri, but I believe she's ready to head toward the air-port."

Ryan hugged Matelda Donatelli, Terri's mom, and shook her dad's hand. From amidst an enthusiastic crowd of well-wishers, Terri emerged with a single carry-on attached firmly to her shoulder and dragging a Pullman. A pint-sized nephew dragged another suitcase behind her.

"So glad you're here." She glanced about with a pasted grin and added, "I need quiet and space."

He laughed and brushed a kiss across her cheek. He would have kissed her on the lips, but the whole family was watch-ing.

"Do you have everything?" her mother asked. She held a huge checklist in her hand.

Terri continued through the door. "Yes, Mom, you checked my suitcases twice. I'm prepared for any emergency known on the face of the earth."

"Mount Vesuvius might erupt," her mother said.

Ryan held his amusement. Once they drove away, Terri closed her eyes and leaned her head back against the headrest.

"Why didn't I choose a weekday to leave?"

"Because you didn't want any of them missing work."

They laughed as though the two were headed out for a sun-filled day rather than a month-long separation by the Atlantic Ocean. The sobering thought reminded him of his parting words to her.

"I have a few things I want to say." Ryan punched off the radio.

"Is this a lecture, Professor?" Her words hinted of sarcasm.

"Possibly. Would you like to hear my version of Hamlet?"

"No thanks, but let's get this over and done."

"Simply stated, I want you to have a good time. I want you to see and do all the things you've dreamed about. Leave no rock unturned. Make a million friends. Take a ton of pictures and download them to me at night — if you have the time. Soak up the Mediterranean sun and swim in the Grotto. Pick a few lemons and buy some souvenirs."

"Why thank you, Ryan." Her gaze registered surprise. "How sweet."

"I have a reason."

Her eyes widened.

"I love you, and I don't want you to have any regrets when you return."

Terri failed to reply but stared ahead at the road.

"Unless you don't plan to return."

Chapter 2

Terri stood on the long dock at Naples waiting for a boat to transport her to Capri. In the early morning, she munched on a cold, hard roll and sipped on the strongest coffee she'd ever tasted. She inhaled the smells of the sea and locked it into memory. Back in Louisville, she'd have tossed the roll and dumped the coffee, but here in the land of her dreams, she savored every bite and repeatedly told herself the coffee tasted of old world atmosphere. Her friends would have laughed at the unsavory meal arising out of years of saving for this trip.

Terri could barely contain her excitement. She'd arrived in Naples yesterday about noon, but the Capri tour group didn't leave until Monday morning for the island. This gave her time to convert money into euros and journal about her flight from Louisville. She'd managed a walk with a couple bound for the same tour and even shared dinner with them.

To think, in an hour she'd be in Capri. Excitement spiraled up and down her spine. If the water didn't look so choppy, she'd be tempted to swim. The tour guide, Lisa, suggested taking motion sickness medication, but Terri ignored her warning. She'd never had a problem before, and her enthusiasm refused to allow anything to dampen her adventure.

She finished the roll and placed her hand over her shoulder bag while glancing into a sea of faces that represented many nationalities. Pickpockets roamed the area, and she anticipated keeping everything she'd brought.

The warm Mediterranean air bathed her face in a mixture of light sprays. Sea gulls dived and soared ahead, now and then grabbing up a piece of crusty bread. Great-grandmother had once been here. She might have stood on this very dock and waited anxiously for a boat en route to Capri. The turquoise-colored water welcomed Terri to a world unlike she'd ever seen, only imagined. Like her great-grandmother, she would live the island's magic.

People began to board the double-decked boat for the approximately forty-minute ride to Capri. Terri shuffled her baggage in line. All those ahead of her left their luggage below on seats then ventured to the open top with its fabulous view. She stood below for a few minutes, wondering if someone might steal her bags, but when everyone hurried upstairs, she followed them. A few of the passengers headed for something to drink, but she didn't want to waste a single moment.

Finding the perfect seat with a wondrous view of the island in the distance, she eased down, allowing the wind to tease her face in a refreshing expectancy of the days ahead. In a few moments, Lisa sat beside her.

"So, do I get a firsthand report of our arrival to Capri?" Terri asked. She had quickly warmed to the darkly tanned young woman from the Bronx.

"I'm up as high as I can be in hopes my motion sickness tablets work." Lisa touched her stomach. "Every time I take this ride, I never know if I'll feel like quitting my job when we dock."

Terri frowned. "You must have a queasy stomach."

"Don't tell me you didn't medicate yourself."

"I didn't see any point in it."

"Take my word, this trip is unlike any you have ever experienced."

A strange fluttering flitted across Terri's

stomach. The boat lunged ahead before she could conjure an intelligent reply as to why she'd ignored the warnings. "I may live to regret it."

Before long Terri vowed to adhere to every suggestion Lisa made for the remainder of the trip. The boat jumped over choppy water that left her hard roll and coffee somewhere in the Mediterranean depths. Still, she attempted to tune her senses in to the first glimpse of the island, a towering mountain rising in a blue-gray and silver haze.

By the time the boat reached Capri forty-five minutes later, Terri trembled with the assault on her body. Next time, she'd water-ski.

Nothing compared to seeing the island for the first time — even if she felt greener than the lush grasses and really wanted to crawl into bed. The island's dock was walled up against the mountain, which meant the boats coming and going used only one side.

"Are you going to be okay?" Lisa placed her arm around Terri's shoulder. "I'm a bit wobbly inside, but nothing like you look." The brunette had a unique accent, which amused Terri despite the current status of her body.

"Thanks. I had plans to enter the local beauty contest this morning." Her attempt at humor sounded flat.

"I'm normally encouraging, but don't spend any of the winnings yet. We'll get to the hotel, and you can rest a little before we start our afternoon activities."

Terri closed her eyes. "Remind me of what we're supposed to do."

"A train ride straight up to a level where we catch a bus to Anacapri. The island is known for its steep hills and narrow winding roads."

Terri tossed her a wry smile. "I'm sure I'll enjoy it."

Lisa patted her shoulder then pointed around the upper deck. "You are not the only one who's had a rough time. We'll linger in the shops and restaurants for awhile until everyone feels better."

Terri nodded. If Ryan had been there beside her, he'd have done everything but thrown up for her. He'd also have insisted she take the motion sickness medicine back at the Bay of Naples. Right now he was sleeping peacefully in his condo in Louisville. Odd how her thoughts turned to him, when she wanted to concentrate only on her vacation.

With Lisa's help, Terri secured her luggage and hobbled off the boat. She wound her way through the various shops, side-stepping the restaurants, and making a mental note to sample the *gelato* — Italian ice cream — when her stomach settled.

When she took the time to study the other tourists, she saw all of them had at least one companion to share the adventures. For a brief moment, she felt a twinge of regret in not having Ryan beside her. But she had Great-grandmother's letter in her shoulder bag, and God promised to never leave her or forsake her. Terri and Lisa had established a friendship of sorts, and a small group of college girls had included her in their conversation. Terri didn't have the heart to tell them about her professorship at Louisville University.

"The train leaves for Anacapri in thirty minutes," Lisa said. She left Terri and the college girls, who introduced themselves as Tami, Heather, and Ashley, outside a bakery while making a round to notify the rest of the group. The scent of fresh bread didn't hold its normal appeal.

Terri scrutinized the train and the track ambling up the side of the mountain. Again her stomach protested. Forty-five degrees up looked precarious. Terri knew about the mode of transportation, but at this particular moment all she wanted was level ground. The seats inside the train were positioned in such a way that the angle of the train did not affect the passengers — a pleasant surprise. The higher the train climbed the more she could see the water and the many lemon trees. Ten minutes into the incline, the passengers moved from the train to a bus. Lisa had been correct in her description of the narrow, winding roads. At each curve, the bus honked to alert any vehicles traveling in the opposite direction.

Repeatedly, Terri told herself she would grow accustomed to the island's transportation, especially if she chose to stay permanently.

"The bus will drop us off at our hotel. It's the second stop on the left past the statue of Augustus Prima Porta," Lisa announced to the tour group. "This statue portrays Augustus as a victorious general posed in the ancient Roman fashion of delivering a speech. Note his stance and body proportions are to reflect an ideal man, athletic and commanding."

Terri remembered from the brochures that this statue was a common sight in Italy. When it came into view, she felt the old excitement tug at her senses. Would the hotel be even more beautiful than the travel brochure depicted? Suddenly a list of all she wanted to see and do toppled across her mind: the villas, the Faraglioni, a yacht tour of the island, Mount Solaris, the Blue Grotto, the churches, and so much more. She yearned to speak Italian to the handsome people living in Anacapri and to delight in the easy lifestyle — so many memories to make in one month's time, and perhaps for a lifetime.

The breathtaking view from the hotel confirmed her trip — twisted rock and cliffs, patches of green, picture-perfect water. She snapped picture after picture, especially the view of Mount Vesuvius from her balcony. Later she'd download the pics and E-mail them to her family and Ryan. He had a special interest in volcanoes, and the story of Pompeii had always fascinated him. The eruption occurred in 79 A.D., and now two million people lived there — not her idea of the perfect home site.

Terri caught her thoughts in a gasp. Why did Ryan have to enter into her magical world? She'd left him in Louisville where he belonged. For that matter, she had no idea what her feelings were for him and didn't care to analyze her heart while on vacation. A moment later, his picture flashed across her mind. She did care for him and at times believed she loved him, but he was a boring English professor. Terri couldn't help but believe her great-grandmother would have insisted upon more.

She stepped into the open hotel onto a turquoise-tiled floor. It reminded her of the sea waters against walls and tall ceilings of white. Her room was typically European: a little small, a tiny bathroom, and no air conditioning. She opened double doors and inhaled the salty air from the balcony. Oh, the glorious atmosphere. Terri didn't need to dream any longer. She could touch, taste, and smell her dream!

Terri felt a need for adventure. Just like her namesake, she desired to experience Capri and whatever it held for her.

Without warning, heaviness pressed against her heart. What did God have in mind for her during the next month? A twinge of fear picked at her, reminding her of a little girl on the brink of opening birthday gifts. What if she didn't receive the treasures she wanted?

The next morning after a breakfast of fruit, hard rolls, and strong coffee, Terri and the tour group headed for a lift that would take them to Mount Solaris. From the moment she began the trek up, the lush green of the hillsides and the lemon trees held her spellbound. At the top, she looked down on Anacapri, more beautiful than her imagination could fathom. Houses dotted the hillside, along with elegant villas, exquisite flowers, and the architecture of centuries old churches — their grandeur invited all to worship. A panoramic view of the water encompassing the bay and Mount Vesuvius rising like a huge cone moved her to click picture after picture. In another view, she captured the Faraglioni rocks, rising out of the water as though they were centurions guarding that portion of the island's jagged edge.

At lunch, the group wandered through Anacapri to sample the local food. Lisa strolled with Terri.

"Where are Tami, Heather, and Ashley?" Lisa asked, gazing at the throng of tourists like a mother hen keeping a watchful eye on her chicks.

Terri laughed. "They found out I'm a college prof. They thought I was closer to their age."

Lisa's mouth curved into a grin. "What a compliment."

"Oh, they're sweet girls, but I made them feel uncomfortable."

"Can I ask you something?" Lisa asked.

"Fire away."

"Why did you take this trip by yourself? And I understand you plan to stay past the week tour." Lisa shrugged. "It's really none of my business."

Terri stood outside a restaurant and inhaled a sundry of enticing foods. The bakeries drew her inside as though the Pied Piper played a tune just for her. "It's a little complicated, but in short, my great-grandmother found the love of her life here, and I wanted to see Capri for myself."

Lisa's eyes widened. "So she met your great-grandfather on Capri, married, and eventually ended up in the States?"

"Not exactly. She was supposed to meet him here but couldn't bring herself to leave her family. They never met again."

"How sad. Did she tell you all this?"

"Yes, and I found a letter in her Bible. It was returned when the man couldn't be located."

"So you came alone."

Terri thought of Ryan and his plan for them to honeymoon on Capri. Irritated at her remembrance, she pushed his face to the farthest corner of her heart. "I'm the daring type."

Lisa studied her curiously. "How about lunch? Are you up for a ham and mozzarella panino?"

"Is that the sandwich with little mozzarella cheese balls?" Terri asked.

"The same, and you'll love the thick wonderful bread."

Late in the afternoon, the group returned to the hotel. Terri had hiked everywhere, and her leg muscles screamed with what the next day would bring. She looked forward to a leisurely bath before dinner. The romance of the atmosphere and anticipation for the evening left her tingling with excitement. Standing in the hotel lobby, chatting with a few of the tour group, she spotted a familiar face.

Ryan.

Ryan knew once Terri discovered he'd made the trip to Capri, she'd be angrier than when she learned her favorite brother had eloped with an Anglo high school dropout. Ryan did not misjudge her reaction.

Fire blazed from her dark eyes. He saw the betrayal, the accusations, the invasion of her Capri escapade. Instead of approaching her, he merely smiled and headed for the elevator. What had once seemed like a wonderful idea now looked like a stunt from a love-struck kid. Humiliation crept up his neck and face.

He stepped into the elevator, but not before Terri scooted in beside him. A middle-aged couple chatted with her, and for the moment, relief washed over his battered nerves. At his floor he exited, and she trailed after him.

"Ryan, what is the meaning of this?"

He whirled around. "I'm on vacation. I figured since I had an empty summer planned, that I might as well check out Capri."

"You followed me here?" Her words fairly exploded.

He pressed his lips together. "Actually, no. Despite what it looks like, I had all the trip information about the island, and I decided to check it all out for myself. I had no idea we'd be staying at the same hotel. For that, I do apologize."

"I don't appreciate this at all." Her face reddened, but when she opened her mouth to say more, a trio of young women interrupted them.

"Hi, Terri. Want to have dinner later?"

Ryan saw her professional façade take

over. "Sure. I want to take a long bath, first."

"Great, how about sevenish?"

Terri nodded and watched them disappear. She whipped her attention back to him. "Are you trying to spoil my day? Are you going to destroy my vacation, too?"

Ryan crossed his arms over his chest. He had never understood Terri's unpredictable, extreme emotions, and this was another one of those times. "Terri, I'm here and I intend to stay." He raised his hand in defense. "I have no inclination of disrupting your vacation. I have my own agenda, which means we will be seeing each other only in passing."

"I don't believe you for an instant."

"That's your choice. I really don't care. You made your feelings quite evident at the airport. I realized in Louisville that you had lost your commitment to our relationship. I'm a single man who has set his sights on a great vacation." He turned to head down the hall toward his room.

"If you plan to act unattached, then I will, too."

Ryan pulled the room key from his khaki pocket. "I never doubted you would do otherwise."

Chapter 3

Terri thought the hot bath would soothe all those things ailing her mind and body, but the fragrant lemon bath salts, native to the island, only relieved the muscular stress, not the choking lump in her throat. Ryan's deliberate plan to ruin her vacation infuriated her. In the next instant, a dull throb developed across her forehead. Did he think she was fool enough to believe he didn't purposely make reservations at this hotel? How could he mask it all by stating he wanted to see Capri and wouldn't get in her way?

I'm a single man who has set his sights on a memorable vacation. She didn't believe those words for one minute. Like a lovestruck puppy, Ryan had followed her half way around the world to keep tabs on her behavior. Even her family hadn't gone to that extreme. She held high expectations for this trip, and she'd enjoy every minute of it no matter his devious interventions. After this, the two of them might not have a salvageable friendship. In fact, she might need to transfer to another university.

How could Ryan betray their relationship like this? For the past three years, they'd been inseparable. They'd laughed together, cried together, celebrated their victories, and prayed through the many trials threatening to separate them.

Terri drew in a breath and held it. They hadn't prayed about this trip. She'd chosen to alienate him from the entire matter. She'd even thought of leaving without telling him good-bye. She'd dreamed of a permanent location in Capri where she might meet the man God intended for her to spend a lifetime.

Terri knew she must pray. Her anger had caused her thoughts to veer in a sinful direction, and her past actions proved deceitful. She needed to ask God and Ryan's forgiveness and to forgive Ryan for attempting to ruin her vacation.

Lord, what is happening here? I don't dislike Ryan. In fact, I care about him very much, but why is he here? Does this look immature to You, or am I overreacting? She took a deep breath. *I'm sorry for the things I said, and I'll apologize.*

With a towel draped around her head and before she applied makeup, Terri phoned the front desk and asked to be connected to Ryan's room. He didn't answer.

Tami, Heather, and Ashley, who Terri had inwardly nicknamed the coed trio, joined her and Lisa for dinner. Like the previous night, the meal consisted of pasta in a tomato sauce, seafood, fresh vegetables, and more of Italy's wonderful bread. Unfortunately, the meal seemed tasteless in light of her tangled emotions.

"Who was that great-looking guy in the hallway?" Tami tossed a lock of platinum hair over her shoulder.

Lisa raised a brow and all attention turned to Terri. She wished she could crawl under the white linen-covered table. Nearby, a violin and soloist crooned a romantic melody, setting a mood for romance. She glanced about the room but didn't see Ryan. He must have elected to eat elsewhere.

"His name is Ryan Stevens, and he's an English professor at Louisville U."

"Where you teach?" Heather asked, a darkly tanned blonde.

Terri nodded.

"Why do I think there's more to the story?" Lisa took a sip of water. "Your face is redder than my sauce."

"Seeing him surprised me." Terri straightened her shoulders. How could she change the topic of conversation?

"So are you two going to hang out together?" Tami asked. Only Ashley, the petite brunette, chose to keep silent.

"No. He has his agenda, and I have mine." Thankfully, the violin and the soloist strode their way, snatching up everyone's attention with a sweet song about a man in love.

At the end of dinner, Terri listened to the others chatter on about the next day's yacht tour of the island. The talk encouraged Terri to push aside her woeful misgivings about a spoiled vacation and look forward to another day.

The waiter, a handsome local wearing a name tag that read Dino, brought them all fresh fruit. He smiled, but he couldn't speak English. Lisa and Terri took turns ordering for them all, and Tami remarked about his perfectly white teeth and model-material smile. Heather stated she'd like to take him home in her suitcase. Ashley merely agreed, while Lisa pointed out the waiter most likely had a new girlfriend each week.

"Let God select the man for you," Terri said. "He already has one picked out for each of us."

"Can't I help Him along?" Tami's blue eyes sparkled.

Terri shook her head and laughed. "I think you're hopeless."

The waiter picked up Terri's uneaten dish of fruit and walked toward the kitchen.

"Excuse me, I'm not finished," she said in Italian.

He didn't hear her and continued across the dining room. Terri rose from her chair and followed him. She tapped him on the shoulder and repeated her earlier statement. Dino flashed a smile that could have melted granite.

"I was teasing you," he said in perfect English. "You and your friends amused me, and I couldn't help myself." He handed her the fruit.

Humiliation crept over her. Terri saw a trickle of silver woven through his thick hair. Handsome did not even begin to describe him. "Thank you." She pointed to her table. "You understand those ladies are going to be mortified once they learn you heard everything they said."

He chuckled. "But I did like what you said about allowing God to pick our life partners. Do you really believe that?"

"Most certainly."

"I do, too."

"Mr. Vitulli?" a waiter asked.

Dino gave the young man his attention.

"Sir, you have a phone call in your office."

He turned to Terri. "Excuse me, Miss. I'm the manager of the hotel. Sometimes I like to work alongside my employees. That way I can appreciate their work. I'll appoint another waiter to your table."

Terri felt her smile coming from her heart to her lips. She nodded and turned to return to her table.

"Miss?" Dino's voice sounded more musical than the violin strings. He stepped to her side. "Since I see you are not in the company of a gentleman, may I ask to see you again?"

Her toes tingled. How long had it been since she'd been noticed by another man? "I think that would be fine."

"Would you care to join me here later on tonight, around eleven?"

Weariness tugged at her, but Terri refused to pass on Dino's invitation. "I'll be here."

Back at the table, she saw her friends once more had their attention fixed on her. This time, she didn't mind. Terri sat and purposely ignored them.

Tami, with her overwhelming sense of curiosity, broke the silence. "I can't stand this. What happened with that gorgeous waiter?"

"Oh, I learned he speaks perfect English."

The three coeds gasped. Words of humiliation spilled from their mouths while Lisa laughed and threatened to tell the entire tour group about the night's antic. Terri couldn't disguise her pleasure with the invitation, but she chose to keep the later meeting to herself. Great-grandmother's letter danced in her memory: Dino, a charming, handsome Italian and a Christian. God had blessed her indeed.

Ryan ate dinner in his room rather than upset Terri with her friends. He'd gone for a long walk shortly after the argument and focused on his motives in coming to Capri. Had he traveled to this isle paradise to make Terri miserable or to win her affections? At this point, he didn't have a clear answer, and it frustrated him. Traipsing to another continent after her sounded like something a sixteen year old would do. At first when the idea struck him Saturday morning after dropping Terri off at the airport, he refused to consider it. By nightfall, he didn't care about the cost or what she might think. He'd planned for months to take her to Capri either as his wife or separately in a tour group. Instead she decided to vacation without him. He'd decided to travel alone and see the sights for himself, even take on a few days in Naples. If they met, he'd deal with the coincidence in a mature manner. Maturity would not get tossed into the sea.

Maybe his stubborn nature stopped him from admitting Terri had hurt him. He loved her with all his heart, and the proof lay in a black velvet box in his carry-on. Why he brought the diamond bewildered him, especially since she'd relayed her feelings for him on the road to the airport. Was this ridiculous venture his last effort to save their relationship?

Ryan couldn't save a one-sided love. With a sigh he stepped out onto his balcony and watched a half moon reflect on the water. In the background he heard the soft sounds of violin music and the hum of low conversations and laughter. He was in Italy, and he had no problem taking in the tourist attractions by himself. But the whole thing made him look foolish — like a stalker instead of a godly man.

All right, Lord, You have my attention. I'll talk to her tonight and apologize. I can easily reroute my trip to Naples and a few of the other cities and not make Terri feel uncomfortable. For certain, only You can orchestrate love between us. I give this relationship to You, where it should have been from the beginning.

Ryan allowed the beauty and the atmosphere of the Mediterranean night to thoroughly relax him. The time escaped him and before he realized it, the clock read a little past eleven thirty. He phoned Terri and hoped she hadn't gone to bed. Her normal metabolism had her falling asleep before nine thirty. She didn't answer, and he didn't feel comfortable leaving a message of this importance. Restless, he grabbed his room key and headed for the restaurant. Maybe Terri and her friends had shared a long, leisurely, dinner. He'd politely interrupt her for only a moment.

Terri gazed into Dino's dark eyes. In a way, he looked like all the men she'd grown up with, and in the next he resembled a storybook version of Prince Charming.

"Tell me about your life in America," Dino said. "I'm curious about your Italian family."

"We are demonstrative, loyal, and loud," she said. "We love each other to the point of a fault, and when we argue, we are just as passionate."

He folded his arms on the table. "Sounds like us here."

Terri wanted to know everything about this kind man. She'd gladly sit here all night and listen to the sound of his voice. "How many brothers and sisters do you have?"

"Ah, you didn't ask if I had any brothers and sisters, you asked how many — the mark of a true Italian. I have two brothers and four sisters."

"And you are the youngest?"

He leaned closer. "How did you guess?"

"I imagine your sisters spoiled you horribly, and you learned how to be charming and manage your own way."

"Absolutely. Now, let me guess. You were surrounded by brothers who protected you from any man who ever showed any interest."

"They still do." A giddy feeling enveloped her.

"I don't blame them." Dino picked up his water glass. "If you were my sister, I'd have guarded you with my life."

"Dino, there's no need to pour on the flattery. I may be an American Italian, but still Italian."

He acted as though pained and patted

her hand. She lifted her gaze and saw Ryan across the room. He stood at the entrance of the dining room, while she and Dino shared a table for two tucked away under an alcove. Luckily, the room appeared deserted. She expelled an inward sigh, but too late. He spotted her. In the dim lighting, she couldn't read his green eyes, but the emotions wafted through the air. She'd most certainly hurt him — again.

She turned her attention back to Dino with Ryan's drawn face playing before her. This was Ryan's fault; he should have stayed in Louisville. Between dinner and the meeting with Dino, Terri had convinced herself the relationship had long since died. She and Ryan could have avoided this if she'd insisted upon closure last Saturday. Reality checked in. This wasn't all Ryan's fault; she'd deceived him and needed to apologize.

"Does your tour guide have big plans for you tomorrow?" Dino scooted back his chair and gestured for a waiter to check on Ryan.

"The Blue Grotto and a yacht tour in the afternoon."

He nodded as though approving the plans. "The Grotto is quite beautiful. Sometimes, when I'm not too busy I swim there in the late afternoon, like a tourist. The water is incredibly clear, almost hypnotizing." Observing the waiter escort Ryan to a table, Dino moved around to face her again. "Would you like to have dinner tomorrow night? About nine? We could eat here or in my private quarters."

Having this wonderful man all to herself tempted her, but Terri cautioned herself against a made-for-order entrapment. "Nine, and here would be fine."

"Good. By then, I will have extra help for the busy evening."

Relieved, she urged the trembling in her body to cease. She'd been with Ryan too long, and the business of getting to know someone else made her nervous. Terri yawned and felt herself redden.

"My lovely lady is tired and needs her rest. Let me bid you good night so you can be refreshed for tomorrow." Dino stood and reached for her hand.

It suddenly occurred to her that she and Dino would pass right by Ryan's table. A wave of guilt assaulted her. She'd betrayed him! Should she greet him like an old friend? Stop and chat for a brief moment? Introduce him to Dino? She cringed. She refused to be rude, but what should she do? Terri attempted to form a semblance of proper words, but just as she and Dino passed by his table, Ryan turned his attention in the other direction. Relieved, she moved toward the elevator where Dino charmed her with an endearing smile.

Terri adored the dimples on Dino's right cheek and his impeccable manners. Her stomach did a little flip. How long had it been since she felt this way about Ryan? Granted Ryan opened doors and displayed a special sentimentality that she appreciated, but he wasn't a handsome Italian and Dino wasn't a boring English professor. Ryan even owned a tweed jacket with leather elbows.

She fairly floated to her room. Words and laughter lingered in her ears. Once inside the confines of her Capri palace, she wondered how her heart would ever stop racing long enough to sleep. Readying herself for bed, she remembered the apology she owed Ryan. A glance at the clock revealed the lateness of the hour. Tomorrow, she'd talk to him. As her body relaxed and she bordered between reality and the dream world, the phone rang.

The shrill sound alerted her senses and woke her instantly. Reaching into the darkness, she answered on the second ring.

"Terri, I know it's late, but I need to apologize."

Ryan. "About what?"

"This trip."

"So you admit you followed me?"

"I'm not sure. It's not how I planned things . . . but I don't want to go into all that now. I want to reiterate my earlier statement. I will stay out of your way."

"Thank you." Terri started to say good night, but remembered her own admission of guilt. "I apologize for losing my temper."

"Which time?"

She heard the teasing in his voice and eased onto the pillow. Ryan could find something amusing no matter how dire the circumstances. "Tonight when I first saw you, and my behavior last Saturday when you took me to the airport. Deceiving you about the trip makes me feel . . ." She squirmed. "Feel disappointed in myself. I regret not having a long discussion with you about the whole thing."

"Do you want to break off our relationship?"

Terri hesitated. After deliberating about this for weeks, why did she feel reluctant to end it now?

"Terri?"

"I heard you. Ryan, I don't have an answer. I came here looking for guidance in many areas of my life." She took a deep breath and exhaled slowly. "My inability to give you an answer is not right either. I certainly am not going to ask you to wait while I sort out my heritage and God's will for my life."

"I want His will, too, but you're right. I won't put my life on hold while you find yourself."

The bitterness in his words implied what he felt about seeing her with Dino. He was angrier than she ever remembered, and he had no right. "Don't put your guilt feelings on me. I'm perfectly content." A tear trickled over her cheek. Why didn't she believe her own words?

Chapter 4

The Blue Grotto had enticed Terri since she first saw the pictures from the travel agency, researched the marvel at the library, and searched for more information online. She'd read every word, savored the descriptions, and imagined herself indulging in every drop of blue water. This morning, she shivered in anticipation of the tour.

Terri glanced around the dining room looking for Ryan. She expected him there since he rarely skipped breakfast. A pang of something pricked at her heart, an indefinable feeling that she refused to dwell upon. Nevertheless, it took residence in her heart and instantly zapped her excitement for the day.

By the time the tour group boarded a bus outside their hotel and took the winding road down to the Grotto, she'd captured the enthusiasm from the others and felt better.

"Some refer to the Blue Grotto as a symbol of Capri. I'll let you be the judge." Lisa stood at the front of the bus. "First let me describe what you'll see. It may take a few moments for your eyes to adjust to the cave. The sun shines through the cavern and reflects off the blue water lighting the walls in a blue cast. It is probably the most spectacular experience of the entire island." She grabbed a pole behind the driver as the bus jerked with a curve. "Ancient Romans enjoyed the Blue Grotto, and their statues were found inside. As time went on, the inhabitants avoided the area in the belief witches and monsters lived there. Enjoy your boat ride — the cavern is filled with beauty and history. I assure you that Capri will always bring memories of the Blue Grotto."

"Can we take a swim?" a teenage boy asked.

"Not until after five when the boats are finished with their tours. You're on your own during that time, so feel free to venture back. Let me remind you the water is cold."

Terri planned to take her swim after the tourist group left for the week. Today, she and Heather chose to be the first to enter the water-filled tunnel. They stepped into the rowboat while those behind them waited to climb into the other waiting ones.

"You'll need to lie down to get through the narrow entrance," Lisa said.

"I'm too old to get into that kind of a position," a middle-aged woman said. "You didn't tell us about the inconvenience."

Lisa smiled. "It's only for a moment, and I believe once you're inside, the difficulty with the entrance will add to the beauty and charm."

"You can manage this," the woman's husband said. "I'll be right there beside you."

The man's encouraging words to his wife caused Terri to glance about. His comments sounded like something Ryan would say. Faced with meeting his family and nearly backing out when she learned they headed for a family reunion, Ryan made a point to tell her he'd not leave her side. He kept his word. Terri ended up having a grand time.

The scent of a popular and intensely strong perfume from Heather attacked her senses. Terri sneezed. A bit of regret nibbled at her. Ryan should have been there in the rowboat with her instead of Heather. The coed giggled as they passed through the entrance. Ryan would have stolen a kiss.

Instantly Terri shoved away her thoughts. Being comfortable with a man didn't mean she should spend the rest of her life with him. Ryan fit into her life like an old shoe, when in fact she needed a new one. Tonight she'd share dinner with a delightful, charming Italian man. For certain, she'd never consider Ryan's memory after this evening.

As soon as she rose to a sitting position, the grandeur proved more than blue light illuminating the walls of the cavern. It became an atmosphere of worship. All the other concerns around her faded in the beauty of God's handiwork, as though a writer of the Psalms had used the Blue Grotto to express His creativity.

For great is the Lord and most worthy of praise.

Never had a sight appeared so awesome. An ethereal light — holy and matchless to anything she'd seen before surrounded her. To even whisper might break the moment.

Lord, where are my thoughts? Why have I been consumed with things that do not glorify You? Here within this breathtaking light, I am humbled by Your greatness. Forgive my ugly thoughts about Ryan, and lead me in Your path.

Ryan slept fitfully and rose long before dawn. He ordered the typical breakfast of rolls, fruit, and coffee to his room, and from his balcony he ate and basked in the beauty of Capri's sunrise. No painter could ever bring this mystical isle to canvas; one must live the encounter. Now he understood why the Russian writer, Maxim Gorky, spent a number of years here. Curzio Malaparte, the Italian writer, claimed Capri as a paradise. Ryan felt those words were quite an understatement. Given the money and time, he'd gladly play out his years writing from a villa balcony.

He planned to tour the Casa Malaparte villa later on today and remember every aspect of it for his students. The momentary diversion from Terri might be just what he needed to pull out of this horrible mood.

Normally, a good quiet time with the Lord helped him to see that focusing on himself was a horrible waste of God's time. However, the sinking feeling today had him more baffled. He feared he'd lost Terri, and he didn't know whether to attempt to win her back or assume she'd find happiness with someone else — like the suave fellow in the restaurant last night.

She'd certainly not wasted any time in replacing Ryan.

Whatever had Ryan been thinking when he announced his intentions to conduct himself as a single man? Beginning a relationship with another woman sounded ludicrous, nearly repulsive, from his point of view. The best attitude for him to take came from his parents' era: if you love someone, set them free. If they're yours, they'll come back. Ryan didn't have the saying word for word, but he understood the meaning of it. With this realization, he knew the logical position meant staying away from Terri and not forcing her to make a decision about their fading love.

When Ryan checked into the hotel, he'd picked up the tour guide's schedule. This way he could plan all of his activities and be assured he wouldn't be in Terri's way. She'd have her own itinerary once he returned to Louisville anyway. He didn't want to think about how horrible the days would be while waiting for her to return.

Shaking the despairing thoughts, he studied the tour group's schedule. He could easily seek out the Piazza Umberto today and see for himself why the small, historical square was called the heart of Capri. Along with the stores and cafés, he could visit the San Stefano Church. Ryan had an interest in the churches there, so after grabbing lunch, he could tour them, too.

Enjoying this vacation came from a state of mind — away from Terri.

Lisa encouraged the tour group to mingle along the Piazza Umberto and enjoy lunch on their own. A problem had arisen with the yacht tour, and plans for the rest of the day had been shifted. While in the ancient piazza, they could take in the sights for most of the afternoon. Terri had considered visiting some of the old churches and mentally listed the ones that piqued her interest.

"No matter how many times I take a group here, I always enjoy the Piazza Umberto," Lisa said. She'd worn her hair in a ponytail and with her tanned skin, she looked like one of the locals.

Terri glanced about. "I like the narrow, winding streets, although this all would be nicer if there weren't so many people."

"I agree. Aren't the flowers gorgeous? Makes me wish I could paint."

"I have little talent in that arena — or anything creative with my hands," Terri said. "If I close my eyes, I can picture ancient people going about their daily business, the women with baskets and jars on their heads and children playing about their feet."

"Some scholars claim the walls of these structures date back to one thousand years before Christ and others much later. No one is really sure, but the architecture of the limestone blocks is about the fifth or sixth century."

"You are a walking storehouse of information." Terri laughed. "What do you do in your spare time?"

"Collect stamps." Lisa burst into laughter. "Not really, but I do enjoy fly fishing." She glanced to the right of them. "Isn't that guy staying at our hotel?"

Terri swung her gaze in the direction of the bell tower in the square. The three coeds stood with Ryan. Tami leaned into him and Heather touched his arm. Only Ashley kept her distance, but her tank top dipped short of decent.

Lisa peered at the foursome. "It's embarrassing how those girls throw themselves at guys."

"Right, and he doesn't seem to mind a bit."

"Why, you're angry," Lisa said. "Have you taken those girls under your wing?"

She peered into Terri's face then back at the coed trio and Ryan. "Frankly, I see this all the time."

"It doesn't honor God." Terri stared into Ryan's smiling face. How could he do this to her? Was he flirting simply because he knew she'd watch his every move?

"You're right. I'll have a talk with them later."

"Good," Terri said. "I'm sure their parents would be appalled."

Lisa urged her to walk away from the sight. "Do you have plans for dinner tonight? I thought of eating at a cozy restaurant in Anacapri and wondered if you might want to join me."

Terri toyed with the truth, but what did she have to hide? "I have a date for dinner."

Lisa stopped in the middle of a crowded group of people. "Who? None of the men on the tour seem to be your type, especially since they're all married or too young."

"He's the manager of the hotel."

"Oh. The cute one with the dreamy eyes."

Terri nodded. "We met last night for coffee and he asked me then. You and I can have dinner tomorrow night, if that's okay."

"Sure, but you're avoiding the obvious. Did you speak to him in Italian and sweep him off his feet with your brilliant accent?"

"Are you kidding? I haven't spoken a word of it since I arrived."

"Then tell me how did you get such a handsome guy to ask you out?" Lisa waved her hand. "I didn't mean that. You're a great-looking woman, but what's your secret?"

"He knows a beautiful Italian woman when he sees one."

The two walked beyond the Piazza Umberto, laughing and talking about their lives. Terri fought the urge to turn around and see if Ryan and the coeds were still lingering. The thought of him dating one of those college girls infuriated her.

"Ready to head back to the others?" Lisa asked. "Some of them panic when they can't find me."

During her student teaching, Terri taught junior high. She knew exactly how Lisa felt. Truthfully, Terri wanted to see if Ryan had left the area. The short walk revealed him and the girls still chatting away.

"I've had enough of this," Terri said.

"What?"

Terri didn't reply. Instead she headed straight for Ryan. He was a disgrace to the teaching profession, and she intended to let him know about his inappropriate behavior. She gave her attention to the girls. After all, Lisa planned to handle them.

"Excuse me for disturbing you." Terri pasted on a smile. "May I have a word with Ryan?"

"Oh, hi, Terri," Tami said. "Ryan is so funny and cute, too."

"Actually, he's a great guy," Heather added.

Ashley said nothing. Her scooped neckline spoke for her.

"I'd like to discuss something with you girls," Lisa said, her voice laced with sweetness. "Let's grab something to drink first."

The coeds and Lisa moved toward a café, leaving Terri and Ryan alone. His face displayed no emotion, but she'd known him long enough to recognize the depth of his feelings.

"What can I do for you?" Ryan's green eyes cast yellow flecks in the sunlight. His hair looked lighter, too.

Terri patted her foot against the stone street. "Stop this foolish behavior. I'm embarrassed."

"Why? I'm staying out of your way, and I was here before your tour group arrived."

"I don't believe that for an instant."

Ryan pulled a folded piece of paper from his pocket and slapped it against his palm. "This is your tour group's itinerary. Look at today's schedule; it says Blue Grotto in the morning and yacht tour in the afternoon."

Terri swallowed. Regret began to weave an uncomfortable path through her body. "That doesn't excuse what you've done."

Rarely did Ryan exhibit anger, but lines buried across his forehead and his jaw tightened. "Are you asking me to leave Capri? What's the deal here?"

She closed her eyes. Looking at him only fueled her anger. "The way you threw yourself at those college girls is disgusting."

"I'm not so sure it's any of your business, but they approached me."

"You certainly seemed to enjoy the dialogue."

Ryan nibbled at the inside of his mouth. "Really, Terri, green is not your best color."

Her pulse raced along with her temperature. "How dare you? I'm referring to your reputation. LU might not like the idea of their prized English professor linking up with coeds on an island paradise."

He moistened his lips and studied her face. "I have done nothing to warrant this outlandish accusation."

"Looks to me like you picked up a couple of younger women to make me jealous."

Ryan laughed, an artificial, irritating laugh. "I can't make anyone jealous who doesn't feel anything. And while we're on the subject of immature behavior, what about you throwing yourself at the waiter?"

"That's none of your concern. We are adults who are enjoying a friendship."

"Let me get this straight. You want to control any woman who talks to me, but you can go about your vacation however you wish. Something doesn't sound right."

Terri realized she couldn't talk sense to Ryan. "I was merely pointing out the dangers ahead by associating with naïve young women."

Ryan nodded in Lisa and the girls' direction. "At this point, they are more mature than you are."

Terri wanted to throw rocks at him. She'd merely tried to help him regain his senses. Glancing at Lisa, she hoped her friend had experienced better luck with the coed trio.

"I'm continuing my day," Ryan said. "I

suggest if you want to ensure our paths not cross then leave a note for me at the front desk when your tour guide changes plans."

Chapter 5

Sweat streamed down Ryan's face. His shirt stuck to his back, and he clenched his fists. Never had he been this furious with Terri. First with her obvious jealousy — the only time she'd ever displayed such disappointing emotion — and secondly with what she thought he and those college girls were discussing. Granted young women tended to flirt as much in Capri as they did on American soil, but he knew his stance as a highly regarded professional and a godly man.

The three had questions about the history of Capri. They were part of a two-month tour of Italy as an extension of their college studies. Their knowledge of Mount Solaro and the Piazzetta equaled his. The girls were respectful, and their conversation continued on with the differences in Italian food, drink, and mannerisms. Laughter rose when a small boy and his sister struggled over the ownership of a shiny rock. Then one of the young women mispronounced the name of a villa, and the other two found the mistake amusing.

Ryan felt discretion needed to be taken and excused himself from the conversation. But before he could walk away, Terri approached him with her accusations.

He didn't understand her one bit. They'd agreed the night before to enjoy their vacations separately and now this. Immaturity embedded in his mind. Terri's behavior involved a healthy dose of selfishness. She wanted a dream vacation complete with an Italian escort, while Ryan said and did nothing but act like an eighty-year-old professor. Besides, if she didn't care what he did, then why the show of jealousy?

Ryan stepped into one of the many tourist shops. He wanted to pick up something lemony to take back to his mother, probably bath salts like the ones in his room. He'd heard about the yellow lemon-flavored chocolate, a sure treat for his dad. After making his purchases, he made a decision. Once back at the hotel, he'd look into spending a couple of days in Naples. He wanted an opportunity to check out Mount Vesuvius and a host of other scenic and historical spots in and around the city.

Later on today, when he cooled down, he'd try to talk to Terri about this afternoon. He planned to apologize — again —

for losing his temper. If he dwelled very long on his anger and not his direction from the Lord, she owed him one huge explanation.

Shaking his head, Ryan elected to tour the churches in the area. The one there in the Piazzetta, San Stefano, had its origin at the end of the seventeenth century. He'd already seen the marble inlay floor and the wooden picture of the Madonna and child, which, historically, had been thrown from a cliff by pirates and later found intact. With his interest piqued, Ryan moved on to tour the other churches. Some dated as far back as the Middle Ages. The Church of Saint Maria of Constantinople claimed to be the oldest parish on the island. It dated back to the eighteenth century, but the original church beneath it was built in the fourteenth. Odd how Americans grew excited about historic landmarks from the late seventeenth century, while the rest of the world hailed ancient structures, some built before Christ. Ryan often wondered how the ancient civilizations managed such feats.

Midafternoon found him at the Church of Saint Michele Arcangelo. He studied the magnificence of the tile floor depicting the banishment of Adam and Eve from the

Garden of Eden, painted by Francisco Solimena. From the corner of his eye, he saw Terri and the tour guide slip into the back of the church.

He caught her eye and nodded. She moved his way, and he wondered if she intended to make another scene. Earlier this woman proved not to be the one he loved and cherished in Louisville. Was she about to confirm his earlier findings? What about this beautiful island had transformed her into . . . into someone he didn't know? His miffed feelings returned at the sight of her, but as she neared, all of his resolve to stand up for himself faded.

"Ryan." The sound of her voice sent his heart racing. His heart betrayed him.

Jamming his hands into his pockets, he forced a tight-lipped smile. "I'm just leaving."

"Could we talk?"

"I'm leaving, and right now is not a good time to discuss anything."

She shifted her camera bag and moistened her lips. "About today."

He strode past her. "Not now, Terri."

"I have some things I want to say."

"Not now!"

"You don't need to shout."

"I'm sorry." Ryan nearly bit his tongue,

192

stopping a caustic remark.

"When?"

For a moment he thought he heard the old Terri — the gentle lift of her voice. He whirled around, anxious to see if the light of love still flickered in her eyes. Ryan braved forward. If they shared another argument, perhaps it would be closure for their dying relationship. If they got along fine then he could see hope for the future. "Tonight, around nine or so sounds good."

She sucked in a breath. "I have plans."

The words flew to his mouth before he had time to stop them. "A date?"

Terri's face hardened. "Let's not quarrel."

"You're right. I believe I was leaving."

Terri watched the man she thought she knew walk away. Ryan's back stiffened as he headed to the rear of the church. He greeted Lisa as he left. *Turn around, Ryan, please.* Terri no longer knew the English professor, the calm man who always put her cares and feelings first. Something about this island had changed him into a rude and obnoxious person.

She'd made a little mistake back there with the coeds, and he wouldn't even give her time to apologize. Maybe this was better. At least she found out here and not after a wedding. Perhaps her destiny was here on Capri and possibly with Dino.

Determined to hide the turmoil raging through her, Terri blinked and focused her attention to the front of the church. A moment later she felt a hand on her shoulder.

"Why don't you tell me what's going on? I've got a good ear." Lisa's Bronx accent that had sounded almost comical in the past now offered comfort.

"I can't. I don't even understand it all myself."

"Maybe by talking you can sort it out."

Terri released a pent-up sigh. "It might take awhile."

"Everyone is on their own, remember?" Lisa waved her hand around the church. "We're in the perfect atmosphere for a heart-to-heart talk, and when you're done, we can pray about the problem."

Terri crossed her arms and paced across the tiled floor. Tears threatened to flow, and she wasn't sure if they were for her or the lost relationship with Ryan. She thought she could trust Lisa, believing God must have put her in Terri's path for a reason.

"Let's sit down," Terri said. "This may take the rest of the day."

Without a word, Lisa acquiesced, and they slid into a pew.

"Before you begin, I'd like to ask the Lord to bless our time together," Lisa said. Without waiting for a response she began. "Heavenly Father, something has my friend upset. I want to help her work through this. Please use me to bring her to an understanding that You love her and want the best for her, amen."

"Thanks." Terri took a deep breath. "I've known you for only a few days and I'm about to reveal things I wouldn't want my own mother to know."

"Whatever you say goes no farther than me."

Terri considered the situation for another moment then plodded ahead. "Ryan and I have dated for the past three years. We've talked of marriage, but nothing has ever been mentioned about love — sort of like the cart before the horse. I didn't tell him about this trip until right before I came. Needless to say, that was wrong."

"Then he shows up here."

"I hurt him badly, and I apologized, but he doesn't really understand why I came to Capri alone."

Lisa took her hand. "Was this your way of breaking off the relationship?"

"Maybe . . . I'm not sure. I thought my trip was to be a part of my great-grandmother's legacy, but now I'm rather disgusted with myself." She focused her attention on Lisa, hoping the truth might resurrect in her friend's eyes.

"Are you expecting to meet the man of your great-grandmother's dreams?"

The perpetual lump in her throat grew bigger. "I wish I knew. This sounds horrible, but I just wanted to do what she couldn't. Now hearing myself say the words makes me sound childish and foolish."

"Pardon me, but Ryan sounds a bit childish, too."

Terri hesitated. "He said he'd already looked into the trip for this summer either as a honeymoon surprise or the both of us booked separately in a tour. I blew his plans."

Lisa nodded. "So he came anyway."

"Yes, but he says he came because he'd already planned it. In fact, he's carrying around our tour group itinerary so we don't cross paths." A tear slipped down her cheek. "I'm not sure what to believe."

"Do you love him?"

How often had she asked herself the same question? "I'm not sure about that, either. When I left him at the airport back home, I couldn't get away fast enough, but —"

"But today you overreacted when you saw him with Tami, Heather, and Ashley."

"I was really out of line. I must have made him furious, because he wouldn't even let me attempt an apology." Terri's stomach churned. "Looks like I want to have this fabulous vacation, and when it's over I can decide if I want to spend the rest of my life with Ryan."

Lisa said nothing.

Terri leaned back on the pew and massaged aching neck muscles. "I'm pretty despicable. My actions don't say much for my value of him or God."

"So what do you want to do about it?"

"I want to tell Ryan I'm sorry, but from there I don't know."

"Do you really want to find out what God wants?"

Terri stiffened. "Of course! I haven't slid that far back."

"Are you still having dinner with Dino?"

"Absolutely."

"I don't advise going, unless you're sure you don't have feelings for Ryan. It's not fair to either of them if you're undecided."

Terri felt the liquid emotion flow freely. She buried her face in her hands. "How can a Christian, educated woman like me be so torn with her life? I really want to have the dinner."

Lisa hugged her shoulders. "I think it's called distraction."

Lifting a tear-glazed face, Terri sensed the conviction in her spirit. "Instead of dinner with Dino, I need to spend time with the Lord."

"I think that's a splendid idea."

Terri peered at the altar. How many other people had graced this church, looking for answers? Love seemed so complicated, especially when it meant a commitment for life. "Oh, Lisa, how could I ever think a fairy tale romance with someone I didn't know could compare with what God has planned for me? I don't know if the man for my life is Ryan, but I'm not doing one more thing until God gives me direction."

"Good. I need to get back to the bus soon and check on the rest of our group. Do you want to come along or stay here awhile longer?"

Terri expelled a heavy sigh. "I believe I'd like to sit here. I can always take a taxi if I miss the bus."

Lisa rose from the bench. "I'll see you soon."

"Thanks. Do you always counsel your tour group?"

Lisa smiled. "You'd be surprised."

"If you see Ryan, would you tell him I really want to talk — anytime he chooses?"

Lisa agreed and departed from the church. The quaintness of the centuries-old building left Terri feeling peaceful. *God, You are here with me, aren't You?*

She didn't expect an answer, but she did feel the incredible love surrounding her.

Forgive my childish ways. I'm ashamed of my actions and how I've hurt Ryan. Lord, if he is the one for me, please tell me. Right now, I don't even know if he'd forgive me for the hurt I've caused. I pray for the right words to convince him of my sincerity. Thank You, Lord, for always loving me — even when I'm not loveable.

Terri studied the tile floor. How fitting for her sin — Adam and Eve cast from the garden of paradise into a world that would battle against them to the day they died. In retrospect, Capri held the title of paradise, but the likeness didn't mean sin had escaped the island. Real paradise came only from God, whether the believer emerged from the slums of a large city or a tropical isle.

When Terri left the church an hour later, she flagged down a taxi to the hotel. Once inside, she promptly gave her regrets to Dino.

"Can we reschedule? Perhaps tomorrow night is more to your liking." He tilted his head, as though crushed beyond imagination.

"Dino, I wouldn't be good company."

"Ah, the problem must be another man."

Terri hesitated. "Yes, it is. I hope you understand."

He took her hand into his. "Affairs of the heart, we Italians always understand, but if you change your mind, you know where to find me."

Terri's next order of business came in contacting Ryan. He neither answered his phone nor his door. She double-checked every possible area of the hotel property, but nothing. Ryan often spent time on long walks at home, which gave Terri some consolation. Yet apprehension gripped her heart.

She left another message on his room phone about ten o'clock. When only silence greeted her, she decided to write him a note and slip it under the door. After midnight, Terri went to bed, tossing and turning until the brilliant Mediterranean dawn moved her to the balcony.

Oh, Lord, have I ruined things? Have I hurt him so badly that he can't bear to hear my voice? I can't blame him, but I'm begging for a chance to tell him I'm sorry.

Chapter 6

Terri pulled out her great-grandmother's Bible. In her haste to pack, she'd neglected to bring her own English translation. How sad, for Terri's Bible had notes written in the margins and several passages underlined.

Picking up the worn book, she searched through the Psalms. After reading several and praying the verses aloud, she turned to the front and stopped at I Kings, chapter nine. She had no idea why the accounting of Solomon's reign captured her attention, but suddenly she became immersed in the story. In the beginning of his rule, Solomon honored God with obedience to His commands. As the news of his wisdom spread, he accumulated more wealth than any man before or after him. Terri read on through chapter ten, silently cheering King Solomon and his fame — all because of his love and respect for God. Chapter eleven started out with the beginning of his downfall. The king had seven hundred wives and three hundred concubines. By the end of the chapter, King Solomon had sunk to great deprivation. He allowed his wives to manipulate him into serving other gods.

Terri closed the Bible and wondered why the story had held her interest, unless it served as a distraction from the turmoil going on around her. She pondered the similarities of Solomon's downfall and her desire to forget her problems. It all summed up in one word, the same word spoken today in her conversation with Lisa. Distraction.

A fluttering in her stomach caused Terri to once more focus on Solomon. He'd become distracted with the desires of his pagan wives. As a result of not following God's commands, his family eventually lost the kingdom.

Did Solomon's sin have anything to do with her? Had she been so preoccupied with great-grandmother's letter that she neglected to see God's blessings? She massaged the shivers on her arms. The thought of losing Ryan permanently frightened her. She'd literally run him off with her self-centered ways. When she compared his good qualities to his bad, an unbalanced scale set in her mind. So what if he taught English? Ryan's excellent mind and superb teaching skills earned him national acclaim. He might not have said he loved her in the conventional way, but he proved it with his endless devotion. Not that Ryan suffocated her. He'd always stood in the background and silently tended to her needs.

I've been such a fool. Lord, forgive me.

An hour later, she gave up on Ryan returning her call.

"Ryan Stevens checked out yesterday afternoon," the clerk said.

Terri felt the bottom roll out of her stomach. "Did he say where he was going?"

The clerk looked at her like she'd asked when Mount Vesuvius would erupt. "Not to my knowledge."

"Thank you." Terri trembled and turned away. "Did he leave any messages?"

The clerk studied her closely. No emotion creased his face. "No. Nothing."

"May I talk to the desk clerk who checked him out?"

"I personally took care of Mr. Stevens."

Disheartened, she thanked him again and headed to the elevator. In exactly twenty minutes, the bus pulled out of the hotel with the tour group en route for the yacht tour. She couldn't go, not with this news.

Lisa met her at the elevator. "What's wrong? You were in much better spirits at breakfast."

Terri lifted her chin, determined not to cry. "Ryan checked out of the hotel yesterday afternoon."

Lisa sucked in a gasp. "Oh, Terri, I'm so sorry."

"I had this big speech prepared. I was ready to beg and crawl for his forgiveness."

"I'm sure he's somewhere on Capri. You could try calling all the hotels after we get back."

Terri's mind raced with the possibilities. Ryan had always been predictable, until he came to Capri. "You don't think he decided to head home?"

Lisa glanced around the hotel lobby before answering. "You know him better than I do. I'd rather think he's staying at another property."

"What do I do now?" Terri asked. "I'm confused and miserable."

Lisa linked her arm into hers. "Join us on the yacht tour. You can try to locate him later."

"I think I should stay here and make calls."

"And I think you should be with people and not alone."

The elevator door opened and the two women stepped inside. "Get your things and meet me at the bus," Lisa said. "This is a beautiful day and no one should be shut up inside —"

"Feeling sorry for themselves?"

"Exactly."

Ryan grabbed his luggage and lined up behind the passengers at Capri's dock. After yesterday, he wanted to get away from the island and never set foot on it again. All this trip had done was prove him short of insane for following a woman halfway around the world who didn't want him. He'd spent money that could have been used for something else instead of a useless trip to an island paradise. This was once designated as a honeymoon. Who ever thought a honeymoon came in singles? Stupid, purely stupid. All this time, he'd kept kidding himself about the real reasons for hopping on a plane and flying to Italy. His dad was right; men did crazy things because of women. At least being a boorish professor had kept him sane.

He could have taken the money spent on this trip and the two-carat diamond and purchased a new car — without all the heartache. Ryan stiffened. He could have pursued another Ph.D., added hardwood floors to his house, donated the money to a third world country with people starving to death, given it to church, anything, absolutely anything, besides blowing it on a woman who didn't care a whit about him.

An attractive redhead flashed him an ineffable smile. *Don't even bother, Lady. I'm finished with women unless God plants one in my front yard wearing a sign that says, "I'm Eve and you're Adam."*

"Are you traveling alone?" the redhead asked.

"Yes." Ryan tugged on his luggage. He refused to look at her.

"Spending time in Naples?"

"Yes." He scratched his whiskered chin.

"Alone?"

"Yes." With his final reply, he dumped his luggage on a lower seat and made his way to the upper deck. The last trip on these rough waters hadn't bothered him, but he'd again taken the recommended motion-sickness medicine. Right now he didn't care if the whole crew witnessed his dissatisfaction with the Mediterranean Sea.

Bitterness isn't a sign of a godly man.

Ryan found an empty seat and plopped down. He hated being reminded of his sin.

Love is patient.

He knew all that. The passage came from I Corinthians thirteen. He felt a nudge against his spirit to read the verses, a shove to read it right then. Ryan reached inside his carry-on and fished his way through his camera, passport, lip balm, sunscreen, and travel brochures to his New Testament. While the boat jolted and jumped, he read and reread the definition of love.

Love is patient, love is kind. It does not envy, it does not boast, it is not proud. It is not rude, it is not self-seeking, it is not easily angered, it keeps no record of wrongs. Love does not delight in evil but rejoices with the truth. It always protects, always trusts, always hopes, always perseveres.

In short, love was unconditional. Taking a deep breath, Ryan decided to do some heavy-duty praying while this boat bounced across the waves to Naples. The ride couldn't twist and turn his insides worse than his spirit felt.

Once he docked at Naples, he realized the futility of harboring bitterness against Terri. That type of sin promised to fester in him, with a guarantee of making him an angry, resentful man. Forgiveness was in order . . . soon. Although he hadn't gotten to that point yet — he wanted to be there. Until then, he intended to focus his thoughts and spirit on cleaning up his heart.

Stubbornness was not a godly characteristic either.

Ryan tugged on his luggage and waved down a taxi driver. He loved Terri and didn't expect those feelings to vanish. Tonight he intended to rest and take care of a little matter between himself and God.

The following morning, Ryan phoned Terri's hotel, but she'd already left with the tour group.

"Has she left a message for Ryan Stevens?" he asked.

"No, Sir, but she does know you checked out."

Ryan's heart plummeted. "Would you connect me to her room?"

A moment later, the beep sounded for him to leave a message. His initial goal to sound strong and in control squeaked out like a weak monotone. "Hi, Terri. I'd like to talk to you at your convenience. You can reach me in Naples at . . ." Ryan searched the phone and the pamphlets around the room, but couldn't find the number. Before he could finish, his time expired. Frustration picked at him. He called the front desk of his hotel, but the clerk couldn't speak English. With a deep breath, he phoned Capri to leave another message. "Hi, Terri. Would you believe I can't find the number here at the hotel? And the front desk attendant doesn't speak English. I need you here to translate." *That wasn't a smart thing to say.* "Anyway, I'll try your room later." He disconnected then palmed his hand against his forehead. He still hadn't said what he intended. One more time, he dialed Capri.

"May I have Terri Donatelli's room please?"

"Most certainly."

Ryan waited until he realized his phone charges would equal the national debt.

"I'm sorry, Sir, but I'm unable to connect you to her room. Our phone system is experiencing problems. Can you please try back later?"

Ryan replaced the phone as gently as his rising temper would allow. He remembered Terri stating how he never grew intensely angry or charged up with enthusiasm. Something about Italy had pushed that characteristic over the top.

He snatched up his camera and headed downstairs. This would be a perfect time to visit the site surrounding Mount Vesuvius. He and the volcano, which had erupted more than fifty times since it first destroyed Pompeii and Herculaneum in 79 A.D., were sleeping time bombs. Luckily Ryan found strength in the Lord to control his new-found anger. Although the thought of God racing after him with hot volcanic ash at the speed of a hundred miles an hour did make him feel a bit warm.

Thank You for hearing my confession last night, Lord. I know the situation between Terri and me will work out according to Your perfect will.

Ryan boarded a bus and headed toward Mount Vesuvius. He'd been interested in the volcano since childhood, mostly because of the excavation of Pompeii. It puzzled him as to why two million people now lived in the area, as though challenging the mountain to shower them with ash, stones, and pumice while ushering in a river of molten rock. He remembered excavators finding bread in stone ovens preserved for over two thousand years. Right now he felt like his unconfessed sin had hardened for that length of time.

He shivered. Looked like God had a good reason for paving the way to Italy. Back home, he wouldn't have noted the analogies.

He toured the Museo Archeologico Nazionale, one of the greatest museums in the world, housing many of the relics of Pompeii and Herculaneum. The collections captured his attention, but he couldn't rid his mind of Terri.

As soon as he returned to the hotel, he called Capri. Their phone system was still unable to transfer calls. Ryan swallowed the words forming in his mind and thanked the desk clerk.

"Would you like to leave Miss Donatelli a message?"

"No, thank you." He wanted to talk to her personally. Surely by tomorrow he'd reach her. The longer the hours away from her, the more he felt his love grow. Strange, but true.

The following morning, he received the same information. Determined to find patience, he elected to seek out historic churches and take a tour of the catacombs — the underground burial grounds used by Christians in ancient times to escape persecution. Those dank and dark tunnels made him appreciate living in a country that allowed freedom of religion.

In the late afternoon, Ryan tried Capri again. By this time he felt sure the phones had been sabotaged.

"When do you expect the phone system to be in working order?" Ryan asked the clerk in Capri.

"Soon, Sir. Very soon."

Ryan replaced the phone and glanced about his hotel room. Sitting there waiting for modern technology to take control of his forgiveness issue with Terri seemed like having scientists figure out the origin of man. First thing in the morning, he'd take the boat back to Capri.

Chapter 7

Terri listened to Ryan's message repeatedly until she memorized every word, including how he said them. A lot of good it did her since his voice contained no emotion. If only he'd indicated why he needed to talk to her. When he didn't call back, the grueling situation grew worse. She contacted the various hotels, villas, and rental properties to see if Ryan Stevens was registered as a guest, but nothing. Of late, she wondered if he'd gone home. Even with allowing travel time, Ryan should be in Louisville by now. There his phone rang endlessly until the answering machine kicked in, and then she heard this long hum indicating a trail of messages. She'd left two and saw no reason to leave any more. Where could he be?

She considered everything from Ryan using an alias to the possibility he didn't want to hear from her or anyone else. Not that she could blame him.

"You're driving yourself nuts," Lisa said. "If you don't talk to him before you leave

Capri, then you'll see him when you get home."

Terri groaned. "That's what I'm afraid of. This trip means nothing until I can talk to him."

"Girlfriend, you might have to cut your stay short."

"I know, and I'm considering heading back to the States. I'll give him a few more days before I make a decision."

The two women walked into the hotel after a day of touring villas. The styles and gardens were breathtaking, but Terri ached to have Ryan there beside her.

"Miss Donatelli," the desk clerk said. "May I have a word with you?"

Instantly she wondered if Ryan had called.

"A Ryan Stevens has called here several times, but our phone system hasn't been able to transfer calls."

"Did he say anything else, leave a number?"

"No, only that he'd call back later."

Terri's heart sped ahead. "When was the last time you talked to him?"

"On my shift . . . last evening."

"Are the phones working now?"

"Yes," the clerk replied, "as of a little while ago."

Terri seemed to float to the elevator. Ryan repeatedly tried to contact her! The knowledge sent her spiraling upward instead of into the crevice she'd crawled under.

"Okay, so it's good news," Lisa laughed. "Doesn't look like he'll quit trying until he talks to you."

"I'm not leaving my room tonight. Do you want to have dinner with me?"

"Sure. Are you going to be too excited to eat?"

Terri hesitated. "I'm the type who eats when they are up, and this is definitely an up."

Hours later, after Terri and Lisa shared dinner, dessert, and coffee, the phone still sat silent.

"Lisa, there's no point in you babysitting me all night."

"I'm here because I want to be."

Terri stood and paced the room. "You're here because you're loyal and caring. I'm an adult and can handle what does or doesn't happen."

Lisa took a deep breath. "I have a big question, one you don't have to answer, only think about."

"Okay. How badly is this going to hurt?"

"Depends." Lisa stared at her until Terri

offered a brief nod. "You told me Ryan always catered to you — the places you wanted to go, restaurants and things."

"He treated me like a princess, a spoiled one I might add."

Lisa glanced around the room.

"Go ahead. I'm asking for your thoughts. If Ryan and I ever mend our relationship, I don't want to run him off again."

"Do you think you controlled the relationship to the point he basically had enough?"

"Oh, yes." Confused by the obvious statement, she plunged ahead. "I've already admitted to driving him away."

"But why? That's what I think is the core of you and Ryan's problems."

Terri poured herself a glass of water and took a sip before anchoring it on the table. Her mind raced with Lisa's evaluation of the whole situation. "I don't understand. I did everything for him, even told him when to buy me flowers and suggested how his career should proceed."

"My point."

Terri rubbed her temples. She failed to see how Lisa viewed the situation, and it irritated her. Lisa spoke as if she knew Ryan personally, and she didn't. Terri peered into her friend's face. She didn't see any malice, only an earnestness to help. The truth, even more painful than what she'd done, embedded in her mind and latched itself onto her heart. "I . . . I'm a control freak."

"Possibly so."

"You believe control is the issue, not one single incident?"

"Only you and God have the answers."

The ugliness in Terri physically hurt. She wrapped her fingers around the glass of water and brought it to her lips. "I thought I'd worked through all of this, but I haven't." Terri saw where her glass had left a watermark. If she set the glass precisely over it, no one would ever see until the glass moved. The thought was repulsive.

Lisa interrupted her realization. "Are you okay?"

"I don't particularly care for this picture of me."

"Do you want me to leave?"

Terri picked up the glass and viewed the water spot. "Not for the reasons you might think. I need to talk to God about turning everything over to Him. If I don't and Ryan and I come to an understanding, I'll push him away again." She shrugged. "He may have already decided my overbearing personality is too much for him."

"Girlfriend, you can turn the issue over to God tonight, but it could take awhile to change your life patterns."

"I understand. Looks to me like I need to start somewhere and then commit to not falling captive to it again. It makes me sick that I've been trying to play God."

"The reason why He sent Jesus."

A light rap at the door startled Terri. "Yes?"

"It's Tami and Heather and Ashley."

Not exactly who Terri wanted to see, but the girls had been especially sweet the last few days. She opened the door and welcomed them inside.

"We don't want to stay." Tami's gaze darted between her friends and back to Terri. "We just wanted to tell you that we know you're upset, and we hope it's not something we've done."

A lump rose in Terri's throat. "Not at all. Please come in. Lisa and I are talking and we'd love for you to join us."

The girls slipped inside. Heather touched Terri's arm and Ashley offered a smile.

"Really, we don't want to bother you," Heather said, "but we've been praying for you."

All the critical remarks she'd made about the three inched across her mind. "Thank you so much." Terri gestured to the bed. "Have a seat." She noted how Ashley's sundress looked adorable, and told her so.

"Thanks. When Lisa suggested I might not be representing my parents or my college in an appropriate manner, I decided to be more conservative." She reddened. "More importantly, I know God was disappointed."

The girls exchanged looks. "One more thing. You were right about Dino."

She'd been so absorbed in her misery over Ryan that she couldn't remember what she'd said about Dino.

"We're going to wait until God puts the right man in our lives and concentrate on school," Tami said.

It's what I should have done. "What happened?" Terri asked.

"Dino asked each one of us to dinner. We realized he wasn't for any of us."

Suddenly Terri found the admission hilarious. Lisa picked up on the irony of it all, and in the next breath they all were laughing.

"You made my evening," Terri said. "All I've done the past few days is feel sorry for myself."

"Is it the professor from your university?" Ashley glanced at her girlfriends.

Terri brushed back a stray lock of hair. "As a matter of fact, it is." Without considering the matter another instant, Terri told the girls everything. "I'm not such a great person and certainly not a good role model for the three of you."

"But you're transparent," Tami said. "I wish I could so easily confess my mistakes."

"Thanks, but I'll feel a whole lot better when I can apologize to Ryan." She paused. "I've taken advantage of him too many times. Guess I got what I deserved." Terri shivered. "That's not a feel-sorry-for-me attitude; it's simply the truth."

"We'll keep praying for you," Tami said. She glanced at her friends. "We'd better go. I promised my parents I'd call, since tomorrow is our last day on Capri."

Terri reached over to take Tami's hand. "You've been a real blessing. And who knows? If you ever decide to attend Louisville University, you might want to take my Italian class."

After the trio left, Terri turned to Lisa. "You, too, off to your room. I'm fine, really. God's peace came in the way of my new friends."

"Tomorrow's our last day," Lisa said. "We need to make the most of it."

Terri picked up the tour schedule. "Free day. Sounds good. Think I'll take my own personal walking tour and review a few of the villas. Maybe soak up some sun at the pool."

"I have some last minute things to do before I conclude the tour."

"Please," Terri said. "I want us to keep in touch."

"By all means. We'll E-mail and maybe squeeze in a little visiting."

Terri hugged the young woman. "You've been my biggest blessing. Thanks for not allowing me to rot in self-pity, and thanks more for helping me see my faults."

"Absolutely. We're sisters now — just from opposite ends of the country. The next time we meet, we'll work on my head junk."

After tears and more hugs, Lisa left and Terri phoned the front desk to see if Ryan had left a message.

"I'm sorry. Mr. Stevens did call, but we're experiencing problems again."

For the first time, she didn't note the anxiousness. He had attempted to contact her again. His repeated efforts mattered more than anything. She'd make it through this, and if God so desired, the two could mend their relationship. No doubts festered in her heart; she loved Ryan. The thought of hearing his voice sent shivers up and down her arms, and the idea of seeing him again brought emotion to the surface.

I'm in a heavy-duty maintenance mode, God, but I know You will carry me through. A control freak who's out of control. She giggled.

The next morning, Terri took a taxi to the Punta Tragara, a magnificent hotel that some of the members of the tour had visited. After basking in the luscious vegetation along the road, she reached the hotel and its magnificent view of the Faraglioni Rocks. At this height, she could see over their tips. Her mind wandered. The rocky cliffs were forever separated by the clear blue Mediterranean. Dare it not be the case with her and Ryan.

The taxi drove a precarious winding road down to the marina, where she strolled through the throngs of tourists, listening to the romance of the Italian tongue intermingled with the languages of the world. Everyone was in a hurry, impatient to maneuver their yachts into the sea. She observed all those around her. They were too hungry to wait for food; too many people stood in the way to snap the best picture; there weren't enough taxis to take them to their hotel; and there were too many crowded tourist shops. She wondered how long before they stopped to understand Capri's true beauty came in the sense of harmony with God and His nature.

In the moment between the cacophony of the busy crowd and a secret whisper breathing peace in her soul, Terri understood the meaning of Great-grandmother's letter. She also grasped God's purpose in bringing her here to this beautiful island — for Terri to abandon her fantasy world and to mature in her faith. Great-grandmother fulfilled her destiny in marrying a man who brought her to America. He loved her and their children. He took on the role of spiritual leader by becoming a servant to his God and family and establishing a legacy of truth and love. One didn't need an isle paradise to find those things; one only needed to wait for blessings by being obedient and allowing the heavenly Father to control the universe.

Leaving the busy dock, she contemplated a quiet walk with the thought of shortening her trip in Capri. The island's charm held her tightly, but Terri felt a hunger to return to life as she knew it.

"Terri."

At the sound of her name, she whirled around. The words caught in her throat. *Ryan.*

Chapter 8

Ryan saw the varying degrees of emotion pass over Terri's face: surprise, fear, and perhaps regret. He questioned her response. Did meeting him face-to-face cause that much despair?

"I won't take up much of your —"

"I know you've been trying to reach me." Her lips quivered. "Sorry, I didn't mean to interrupt."

He wondered if her abrupt reply was to shorten the conversation. Wouldn't be the first time. "I'm going to finish my vacation touring other parts of Italy, but before I leave I'd like to talk to you."

Terri's face paled. "When did you have in mind?"

"I know you're busy. I'm fairly flexible in my departure."

"Where have you been? I called every hotel, villa, and rental property in Capri."

Startled, he jammed his hands into his shorts pockets. "I was in Naples."

"I thought maybe you returned home."

"Is that what you wanted?"

Tears welled in her dark eyes. "I'm not sure. I don't think so."

"You must believe our relationship is over, which —"

"Ryan."

Frustration bit into his resolve. "Please, Terri, would you let me finish before you interrupt?" He took a breath. "Which is why I need to say a few things. Are you available to listen to what I have to say or not?"

She nodded and a large tear rolled down her cheek. He hadn't expected weeping; although occasionally she resorted to tears to manipulate his actions. This seemed different.

"I'm trying to control the situation, aren't I?"

Her admittance shocked him. "Most likely," he said.

"I can listen now or later. You name the time and place."

"Would you like to take a walk?" His heart picked up pace.

"Yes, and I promise not to interrupt."

He smiled. "You might have to change your heritage."

She returned a shaky smile. "I'll do whatever it takes, and when you're finished, I'd like to talk, too."

Terri's last words touched his heart. He hadn't been deceived; she was sincere. Without a word, the two strolled away from the crowd. "I've been doing a lot of thinking, and I owe you an apology for coming here like a love-struck kid." He expected a response, but she said nothing. "I told myself that I came because I'd planned a trip to Capri for us, and I didn't want the enthusiasm wasted. Truthfully, I chased your plane in hopes of persuading you to marry me. I should have realized you wouldn't have planned this trip without my prior knowledge unless you wanted to end our relationship. For the problems I caused, I am sorry."

He slipped a sideways look at her and saw more tears streaming down her face. Normally she used this opportunity to point out his mistakes. Terri reached inside her purse and pulled out a tissue. Dabbing at her eyes, she peered his way.

"I don't think you caused as much trouble as I did, but if you feel you need my forgiveness, then it's yours," she said.

"Thank you. Now, it's my turn to listen."

Her tears flowed freely, momentarily setting him back. "Terri, I've never seen you like this. Has something happened? Is your family okay?"

"What's happened is the realization of my selfish, controlling nature."

Ryan focused his attention not only on Terri's words but her body language. Could the woman he loved have grown in her relationship with the Lord? She combed her fingers through her hair, and he inwardly smiled.

"Since we started seeing each other, I've called the shots. Really, Ryan, I used the excuse of my Italian family's boisterous personalities to control you and everything we did." She paused and he waited for her to continue. "I feel horrible about this trip — treating you more like a disobedient puppy than a man."

"I'm interrupting here, but I allowed you to manage us. You can't take the responsibility for something when I share the blame."

She reached for another tissue. "I don't know how else to ask this. Are we finished?"

"Do you want to be?"

She burst into sobs. He couldn't bear not comforting her any longer. Gathering his beloved Terri into his arms, he laid her head against his shoulder. "I want another chance," she finally said. Her silky hair fell from the back of his hands; the touch and scent he thought he'd never enjoy again.

"So do I," he said. "I've prayed for this very thing."

She lifted her head. "Really?"

"That's why I kept trying to reach you."

She relaxed and snuggled against his chest — his Terri who never wanted any signs of affection displayed in public. "I will do my best to break my nasty habits."

He chuckled. "Some of them I liked. I do have a suggestion. Could we make our way to the Piazzetta? The church there, San Stefano, sounds like a great place to seek out God. I'd like for us to pray for guidance and His blessings."

"You've never initiated prayer before — other than meal times."

"I'm stepping up to the plate, Miss Donatelli."

She placed a hand on his cheek. "Then swing with all your might."

An hour later, Terri floated on a grand cloud. She and Ryan walked to the Piazzetta and in the quietness of the old church, he prayed. He'd taken the attribute of assertiveness, not pushy or controlling, but one of gentle guidance. She treasured this spiritual side of him. Regret washed away and in its place stood anticipation for the future.

After a talkative lunch, they walked hand in hand through beautiful gardens and villas, although the magnificent structures, vivid colors, and choice greenery could not compare to the love in her heart for Ryan. At one point, she wanted to tell him of her feelings, but feared she might be controlling the moment. This new attitude would take time.

"Where are you staying?" she asked as late afternoon set in.

"The same hotel. I figured if I couldn't get to you by phone then I'd need to come there."

"I'm so glad."

He lifted a brow.

"Really. I missed you so much. Right from the start, everywhere I looked I saw your face."

"How about dinner tonight?" Ryan asked.

"Absolutely."

Soon afterwards, they took a taxi and a bus to the hotel. They visited Lisa by the pool where Tami, Heather, and Ashley sunned. Terri didn't have to explain a thing. Her friends could see the truth in her eyes. Terri and Ryan strolled the grounds, sometimes in silence and other times laughing and talking.

"Are you wanting to rest before this evening?" Ryan asked.

She gazed into his green eyes and watched the afternoon sun cast golden highlights into his amber hair. "I don't want to waste a single moment by being away from you."

"Do you have your great-grandmother's letter with you?"

She startled. "No, I have it memorized."

"Can we sit down? I want to go over everything she wrote."

Confused, Terri agreed. They found a secluded bench among the flowers. With her head on his shoulder, she recited the letter.

My darling Giovanni,

How foolish and wrong I've been. Please forgive me for the pain I've caused you. Believe me, I never meant to hurt you. You brought so much love and laughter into my life, a precious gift from heaven, and all I've offered in return is heartache. You gave me your heart and a promise of a lifetime of devotion. I gave you tears and pleadings for you to join me in Venice. Always I begged for my way until now I fear it is too late. My selfishness eats at my soul; my tears declare my guilt. My joy, my love, I pray you still have feelings for me.

I thought I couldn't leave my family, but God in His infinite wisdom has shown me I can do anything with Him. Giovanni, we can be together, forever as God intended. I love you more than life and I want to live out my days with you. I pray this is not too late.

Visions of Capri are before me. I remember the sound of the waves breaking against the shore, the salty scent of the blue Mediterranean, the cry of the seagulls, and the lure of the mountain peaks. Most of all, I remember your arms around me asking me to be your wife.

Oh, you have captivated me along with the beauty of the island. Please answer me, my Giovanni! I long to be with you. Tell me you still love me!

Feeling a little foolish, Terri couldn't meet his gaze. "I cannot believe I allowed a letter to rule my life for so long. Why did you want to hear it?"

"Ever wonder why the letter was returned?" He wrapped his arm around her shoulder.

"I used to. I really think he must not have loved her after all." She paused. "I will tell you what I think about my great-grandmother's life. She loved my great-grandfather and they had a wonderful marriage, which tells me that was the heart of God's plan."

Ryan kissed the top of her head, the first kiss of the day. "Capri is a beautiful place."

"Being in God's will is the most beautiful place," she said. "I want to go home when you do. Do you mind?"

"I planned to leave in four days."

"Do you mind if I make reservations at the same hotel? I'd love to see Italy with you."

"I wouldn't have it any other way."

Terri lifted her head and he slowly descended to brush a kiss across her lips. "I love you," he said barely above a whisper.

"And I love you."

The food, music, and atmosphere at dinner seemed perfect, or perhaps it was the love in Ryan's eyes that made the evening memorable. The violinist sounded sweet, and when he sang at their table, she nearly wept.

"What are the words to the song?" Ryan asked.

Terri smiled, and as the words graced her ears, she softly translated. "I lost my love, my joy, my all. My heart cried out for peace. Return to me and say you will stay forever in my arms."

Ryan reached inside his jacket pocket. With the shy smile she'd learned to love, he opened a small, black velvet box. Her heart began to pound, and she gasped. He laid a diamond ring in the palm of his hand, the biggest she'd ever seen. In the candlelight, it shimmered.

"You're not translating," he said.

She took a breath and attempted to steady herself. "A life with you is all I ask, a chance to show my devotion. Tell me yes and ease my pain."

The singer stopped. Terri glanced up, and the man smiled. Her gaze swept to Ryan's face.

"Tell me yes and ease my pain," he said.

"Yes," she said, feeling emotion seize control of her heart and mind. "Yes. Yes. Yes."

Dear Readers,

When my son and daughter-in-law returned from a vacation in Italy, they told of their love for the island of Capri. They were captivated by the island's beauty and the warmth of the people as well as the century old structures. Soon, I found myself lost in the stories, the descriptions, the history, the romance of the language, and the photographs. I could smell the sea and feel the cold water of the Blue Grotto. My mouth watered at the thought of pasta and rich coffee. I want you to "visit" Capri. This is an invitation to curl up in your favorite chair and experience the adventure and grandeur of *The Lure of Capri.*

I have been blessed with several novels, novellas, short stories, articles, and devotions. My husband and I live in Houston, Texas, where we are active in our church. My hours are filled with writing, speaking engagements, teaching Bible study, and church librarian. I'm looking forward to hearing from you!

Web site: www.diannmills.com

DiAnn Mills